The Duke's Ruin

KIANA ASPEN

The Duke's Ruin

Copyright © 2025 **Kiana Aspen**

All rights reserved.

No part of this book may be reproduced, distributed, or transmitted in any form or by any means, including photocopying, recording, or other electronic or mechanical methods, without the prior written permission of the publisher, except in the case of brief quotations embodied in critical reviews and certain other noncommercial uses permitted by copyright law.

This is a work of fiction. Names, characters, places, and incidents are either the product of the author's imagination or used fictitiously. Any resemblance to actual events, locales, or persons, living or dead, is purely coincidental.

ISBN: 9798309497720

For inquiries, contact: kianaaspenbooks@gmail.com

First Edition: 2025

For every girl that dreams of a passion that consumes, until then, enjoy Nathaniel.

Chapter One

London hummed with gossip—whispers flitting like restless moths through gilded drawing rooms and over dainty teacups. The scandal sheets quivered with the name of Lady Evangeline Harcourt, her return sending ripples of shock through society. A year ago, she had been the fallen woman, the subject of cruel speculation, abandoned and humiliated after her betrothed, Viscount Nathaniel Sinclair, had been discovered in another woman's bed.

But now, she was back. And not merely as a ghost of scandal, but as the future Duchess of Ashford. Engaged to a man who wielded immense power, wealth, and an influence that even Nathaniel could not ignore.

The whispers reached him before she did. At first, he refused to believe them. That she would return to London. That she would dare step foot into the very society that had torn her apart. That she had chosen another man.

He told himself he did not care. That her return meant nothing to him, that her name no longer carried weight in his heart.

But as the rumours thickened and her presence became undeniable, the truth settled like lead in his gut.

He was lying.

The grand ballroom glittered with excess—diamonds dripping from swanlike throats, champagne fizzing in crystal goblets, laughter curling through the perfumed air like smoke. Nathaniel Sinclair stepped through the towering entrance, his usual insouciance in place, indifferent to the hush that rippled in his wake. He was used to being watched, to being whispered about.

But then he saw her.

His breath hitched. The world around him blurred into insignificance. Only her.

Evangeline Harcourt stood across the room, poised as though sculpted from marble. Her posture was immaculate, the tilt of her chin regal, her expression serenely unreadable. Too serene.

She wore midnight blue, the fabric clinging to her in all the right places, the deep hue making her alabaster skin glow like moonlight. Her beauty had always been undeniable, but now it was sharpened—like a blade honed to perfection. Yet it was not her appearance that unsettled him.

It was the absence of warmth.

The girl he had once known—the one who blushed beneath his touch, who smiled at him in secret gardens, whose laughter had been as soft as a summer breeze—was gone.

This woman standing before him, a vision of icy composure, was not his.

A sharp ache twisted in his chest, unwelcome and unbidden. He had thought himself immune to regret, had convinced himself that what had passed between them had been a mere dalliance, a careless mistake easily forgotten. But the sight of her—this Evangeline who no longer carried even a shadow of the girl he had ruined—shattered that illusion.

She had loved him once. He had been her world, her future, her certainty. And he had thrown it all away for a moment of selfish indulgence, a betrayal so deep it had left her broken and discarded by a society that had once adored her.

And yet, she had risen. Stronger. Colder. Untouched by him in ways that should have soothed his conscience but instead left a bitter sting. The loss was unbearable in its finality.

He had lost her

And for the first time, Nathaniel understood what it was to truly regret.

Nathaniel moved without thought, his body betraying the careful restraint he had sworn to uphold. An invisible force pulled him forward, his pulse hammering against his ribs with every step. He should not approach her. He should turn away, pretend she no longer mattered. But that was a lie, and he had told enough of those.

She stood like a vision of winter, untouched by the warmth of the world around her. The candlelight flickered against her porcelain skin, making her seem almost ethereal. And yet, there was no softness to her anymore, no trace of the woman who had once melted beneath his touch.

"Lady Evangeline," he murmured, his voice even despite the war raging in his chest. He inclined his head in the shallowest of bows, watching her carefully, waiting for something —anything—to indicate she still felt something when she looked at him.

But she did not curtsy. She did not smile. She barely acknowledged his presence.

"Viscount Sinclair," she replied, her tone cool, her gaze impassive. The name cut. Not Nathaniel. Not Sinclair. Just his title, spoken as though he were no more than an acquaintance, a distant memory.

The rejection was deliberate. Razor-sharp. He had braced himself for anger, had imagined her fury, her disdain—a slap, even. He had expected scorn laced with fire, a demand for an apology he could not possibly give.

But this? This indifference? This hollow nothingness?

It was worse than hate.

His fingers curled into fists at his sides, his jaw tightening. He forced himself to keep his expression neutral, though every nerve in his body screamed at him to reach for her, to shake her from this perfect, impenetrable composure. Did she feel nothing? Had he truly lost every piece of her?

Before he could utter another word, a shadow fell over them.

Duke Henry Ashford.

A man of immense power, formidable presence, and the wealth to silence even the most insidious of rumours. And now, the man who stood at Evangeline's side as though he had always belonged there.

Nathaniel forced himself to breathe through his teeth as the Duke's fingers grazed Evangeline's waist, a touch meant as both a claim and a warning. The gesture was practiced, effortless.

Too effortless.

Something hot and venomous curled in Nathaniel's stomach. He remained still, forcing every muscle in his body into submission, but the sight of Ashford's hand lingering on her, the way Evangeline leaned—if only slightly—toward the Duke without hesitation, scraped against his ribs like a rusted blade.

"Come, my dear," Ashford murmured, his deep voice edged with possession. "Our dance awaits."

Nathaniel's breath turned sharp. He watched as Evangeline inclined her head, allowing herself to be led away without protest, without even the faintest glance back.

She did not belong to him anymore.

He clenched his jaw, feeling the grind of his teeth against each other. He had no right to feel this way, no right to the burning, acrid jealousy twisting in his gut.

And yet, as he watched them move together with a

synchronicity that spoke of familiarity, something inside him shattered.

Nathaniel had lost many things in his life. Money. Power. Influence. But none of it compared to the loss of her.

And for the first time since he had ruined her, he realised something cold and cruel.

He had not only broken Evangeline.

He had destroyed himself in the process.

Nathaniel's gaze remained fixed on Ashford as he led Evangeline to the dance floor, his every movement measured and precise. It was the first time Nathaniel had truly looked at the man, beyond the polished mask of the Duke of Ashford—the paragon of nobility, the untouchable figure of wealth and power. And now, watching him so closely, Nathaniel saw what others did not.

Ashford's face was carved into something near perfect—aristocratic features sculpted with precision, his smile effortless, charming. And yet, the closer Nathaniel looked, the more he noticed what lay beneath.

That smile did not touch his eyes. There was no warmth there, no genuine pleasure at being in Evangeline's presence. Only something cold, something predatory.

Nathaniel's fists curled at his sides as he caught the slight press of Ashford's fingers against Evangeline's waist, the grip just a fraction too tight, the way his thumb lingered possessively against the fabric of her gown. She did not pull away, but something in her posture changed—so subtly that no one else would have noticed. No one except Nathaniel.

It was in the way she held herself, the way she turned her head slightly but did not meet Ashford's gaze. The way her breath hitched, barely perceptible but unmistakable to someone who had once known her better than himself.

She was not being courted. She was being controlled.

A flicker of doubt passed across her features. It was gone in an instant, swallowed by the practiced poise of a woman who had learned how to shield herself from scrutiny. But Nathaniel saw it.

And suddenly, the jealousy burning in his gut was no longer just about losing her. It was something else. Something darker.

Just before they reached the dance floor, Ashford leaned in, his lips brushing against Evangeline's ear, his breath a ghost of possession against her skin.

Nathaniel was too far away to hear what was said, but he saw the way she stiffened, the reaction so minute it could have been mistaken for nothing at all. But not by him. Nathaniel had memorised every nuance of her, every instinctive movement, every tell she once carried without knowing. And now, though subtle, it was there—the slightest quiver of her fingers, the way she exhaled just a fraction too slow, as if grounding herself.

The world may not have noticed, but Nathaniel did.

Her expression did not falter, her features a carefully constructed mask of serenity. Yet something in her shoulders tightened, ever so slightly, a breath of hesitation before she allowed herself to be led forward. It was fleeting—gone in an instant—but the weight of it pressed against Nathaniel's chest like a stone.

His jaw locked, his hands curling into fists at his sides.

He had no right to feel protective of her. No right to the coil of unease twisting like a blade in his stomach. And yet, it was there. Dark, insistent.

What had Ashford whispered to her?

And why did she look as though she had just braced herself for battle?

Nathaniel did not leave. He remained rooted in place, his gaze unwavering as he watched them glide across the ballroom floor. His fingers curled into fists at his sides, the fine leather of his gloves creaking under the strain. He had spent a year trying to erase her from his thoughts, drowning himself in meaningless distractions, convincing himself that she was better off without him.

But seeing her now, encased in another man's embrace, ignited something raw and violent within him.

Evangeline moved with practiced grace, each step fluid, each motion impeccable. But there was something missing—something vital that had once defined her. A year ago, she had been radiant when she danced, her joy undeniable, her presence impossible to ignore. Now, she was flawless, yes, but there was no soul behind her movements. No light in her eyes.

It was as though she had been sculpted into a perfect doll, her beauty unchallenged but her spirit absent.

His breath hitched. Had he done this to her? Had his betrayal stolen more than just her trust, but her very essence?

His chest tightened, and for the first time in a long while, he allowed himself to acknowledge the truth: he had lost her. Not simply to another man, but to something far worse. To indifference. To a world where she no longer allowed herself to feel.

And yet, as he watched, something else took root in his gut —a terrible, unrelenting certainty.

This was not over.

Ashford's hand tightened on her waist—just a fraction, just enough to be seen as nothing more than a guiding touch. But Nathaniel saw the truth of it. The subtle claim. The unspoken demand.

Something inside him snapped.

His feet moved of their own accord, carrying him forward with a sharp inhale, his muscles coiling, ready to act. A searing instinct flooded his veins, primal, unthinking. His body had already made the decision before his mind could catch up.

Then—

A fleeting silence. A curious glance from a nearby nobleman, sensing the shift in the air. The prickle of attention from those who knew better than to ignore the sudden, simmering tension between the Viscount and the Duke.

Nathaniel halted. The rational part of him shoved down the instinct, drowning the impulse with sheer force of will. His jaw clenched, his nails biting into his palms as he forced himself still.

He could not do this. Not here. Not now.

But the fire inside him did not fade.

It smoldered, low and insidious, curling around his ribs with the promise of something inevitable. He had tried to stay away. Tried to convince himself that she was no longer his concern.

He had been a fool.

Because every muscle in his body screamed the undeniable truth—

He was not done fighting for her.

Chapter Two

The ball swirls on around him, a grand spectacle of gilded gowns and murmured conversations, of twirling figures and masked intent. But Nathaniel does not move from the fringes. He stands with a glass of brandy in hand, the liquid untouched, swirling absently under the dim candlelight. The music is a distant hum, drowned beneath the weight pressing upon his chest.

Evangeline never looks his way again. Not once.

And yet, his eyes never leave her.

She stands beside Ashford, her posture immaculate, her smile practiced, but Nathaniel sees past the careful façade. He sees the way her shoulders hold tension they never did before, the way her fingers remain delicately curled at her side instead of resting naturally upon the Duke's arm. She moves as though she exists on the edge of something sharp, something unseen.

Then there is the whisper.

Nathaniel replays the moment over and over. The way Ashford leaned in, the brush of his lips against her ear, the way her body turned to stone at the sound of his words. It had been brief, almost unnoticeable. But now, watching the way she carries herself, Nathaniel is certain.

Something is wrong.

He should let it go. He has no right to her anymore.

But the thought coils itself around his ribs, refusing to loosen its grip.

The terrace is bathed in moonlight, the air crisp against the lingering warmth of the ballroom. The scent of roses drifts through the cool night, mingling with the faintest trace of autumn in the wind. Beyond the garden's high hedges, the city hums with distant life, but here, all is silent.

Evangeline stands at the stone balustrade, her hands resting lightly against its smooth surface. She inhales deeply, as though searching for air she cannot quite reach.

Nathaniel steps onto the terrace, his boots near soundless against the marble.

She tenses. She does not turn, but she knows he is there.

"You shouldn't be here," she says flatly, her voice as controlled as ever.

"As if my presence means nothing to you," he murmurs, stepping closer.

She does not answer. The wind lifts a strand of her hair, dark against the pale glow of her skin. He watches the way she remains poised, a perfect marble statue carved into something untouchable. And yet, she is not untouchable.

"Tell me the truth," he presses, voice low. "Are you happy with him?"

She exhales slowly. At last, she turns, her expression unshaken, a mask of effortless indifference.

"Yes."

A lie. He hears it in the measured way she speaks, in the fraction of a second too long that it takes for her to answer. She is testing her own ability to say it.

Nathaniel steps closer, the space between them shrinking

to something unbearable. His voice drops to something dangerous, something almost pleading.

"Did he make you choose him, Evangeline?" he asks. "Or did he take what was left after I lost you?"

Her breath catches. A flicker, a moment of hesitation—but it is gone just as quickly. She lifts her chin, forcing herself to meet his gaze.

"I was never yours to lose."

The words are a dagger between his ribs. His fingers curl into a fist, nails pressing into his palm.

She is shutting him out. Refusing him. Just as she turns to leave, a flicker of movement in the candlelight catches his eye.

At her wrist, just beneath the lace of her glove—a faint discolouration. A shadow against her otherwise flawless skin.

It is nearly imperceptible, something no one else would notice.

But Nathaniel does.

The moment lingers, burning into his mind.

And for the first time, true unease settles deep in his chest.

Nathaniel's blood runs hot.

Before he can stop himself, he reaches out, catching her wrist. His fingers barely graze her skin before she recoils, yanking her arm away as if the mere touch burns. It is not the reaction of a woman scorned, nor one guarding her pride—it is something far worse.

Evangeline gasps, her breath sharp, unbidden. She does not pull away from him, not truly. No—she pulls away from the expectation of something far more dangerous. As though she has been conditioned to.

Nathaniel freezes, his entire body turning to ice.

He has touched her a thousand times before.

Never once had she flinched from him.

Something inside him fractures. A hairline crack in a dam already at its breaking point.

"Tell me who did this to you."

His voice is low, lethal. A demand wrapped in quiet fury. He already knows the answer, but he wants—needs—to hear her say it.

Evangeline snaps back to life, wrenching her wrist free, her expression hardening like steel.

"You don't have the right to ask me that."

She does not deny it.

The silence between them is suffocating, thick with truths neither of them will speak aloud. The truth hovers on the edge of a blade, waiting to tip. He waits for her to break—to yield, just for a moment. But she does not. She refuses him, just as she refuses to acknowledge what he has seen.

Nathaniel forces himself to let it go. For now.

But he is not blind.

Footsteps crunch against the gravel.

Evangeline steps back instantly, her mask slipping into place so seamlessly it makes Nathaniel's stomach turn. The transformation is effortless, practiced—an instinct carved into her by necessity.

Duke Ashford emerges from the shadows, his presence swallowing the terrace in an instant. He moves like a man who owns the world, each step deliberate, every glance carefully measured. His gaze flickers between them, taking in the space that still lingers between Nathaniel and Evangeline. And for the briefest second, something flickers behind his expression.

Possession. Control. Calculation.

Nathaniel forces his features into an easy smile, masking the fury that simmers beneath his skin.

"Viscount Sinclair," Ashford greets smoothly, his tone betraying nothing. "Enjoying the evening air?"

Nathaniel inclines his head, his lips curving into a polite, meaningless smirk. "Quite."

Ashford's smile is sharper, colder. "Good. Though I do believe my fiancée has had enough fresh air for tonight."

He extends a hand toward Evangeline.

She hesitates.

It is no more than a fraction of a second—a beat of silence so small it would be dismissed by anyone else. But Nathaniel sees it. He feels it like a vice around his ribs.

Still, she places her hand in Ashford's, her fingers barely curling around his. It is an act of submission, a silent surrender.

Nathaniel's gut coils in fury, his vision tunnelling at the sight.

Then Ashford leans in, his lips brushing against Evangeline's ear as he whispers something too low for Nathaniel to hear.

Evangeline does not move. Does not react. She merely lowers her gaze, letting her lashes veil her expression.

Nathaniel has seen enough.

And he knows, without a doubt, that this is far from over.

Nathaniel watches them disappear inside, his hands clenched at his sides. His heart is pounding, his mind racing. The rational part of him whispers that he should walk away, that he should accept her choices, respect the distance she has placed between them.

But now, he knows the truth:

Something is wrong.

Ashford is not the honourable duke society believes him to be. There is a darkness beneath his charming exterior, a quiet force of control that keeps Evangeline ensnared. And no force on this earth will keep Nathaniel from uncovering the truth.

His breath comes slow and deep as he turns sharply on his heel, his decision made. He strides into the gardens, the night air crisp against his heated skin, but it does nothing to cool the fire burning inside him. His fists tighten at his sides, his nails biting into his palms as he exhales sharply.

If Evangeline will not tell him what is happening, he will find out himself.

But not yet. Not tonight.

One more confrontation first. One more chance for her to admit the truth. He is not ready to let go—not when he knows she is lying. Not when he knows she is afraid.

The façade may have cracked tonight, but Nathaniel is determined to shatter it entirely.

Chapter Three

Days pass, and Nathaniel forces himself to act as though nothing has changed. He moves through London's social circuit with calculated ease, nodding at familiar faces, exchanging pleasantries with those who still regard him with favour. But beneath the surface, frustration churns like a storm.

He watches Evangeline from a distance at gatherings, studying her every move with an intensity he cannot suppress. She is flawless in her performance—elegant, poised, untouched by scandal. But he knows better. He sees the strain beneath the perfection, the way her smile never quite reaches her eyes.

And then there is Ashford. Always at her side, an ever-present shadow. Nathaniel listens as people speak of him—with admiration, even respect—but their words do not align with the truth he sees.

He sees the way Ashford's hand lingers too long on Evangeline's arm. The way she stiffens ever so slightly at his touch. The way her laughter is quiet, restrained, never free.

Nathaniel clenches his jaw, forcing himself to remain still, to remain patient. He knows she will not willingly speak to him again.

So he must force a meeting.

Nathaniel does not leave things to chance. He bribes a servant in Ashford's household, slipping a hefty sum into the boy's palm for a single piece of information—when Evangeline is alone.

The answer comes swiftly.

She visits the greenhouse each morning, just as dawn breaks, before the household stirs to life.

And so, he waits.

The morning air is crisp, laced with the scent of damp earth and the lingering chill of night. The greenhouse is quiet, the glass panels fogged with condensation as the first rays of sunlight pierce the mist. Nathaniel stands hidden among the foliage, his pulse steady, his resolve unwavering.

Then—footsteps.

Evangeline enters, wrapped in a silk shawl against the morning chill. She moves with familiar grace, but there is something wary in the way she carries herself, as though always expecting an unseen threat.

She pauses. A breath. A shift of the air.

She knows she is not alone.

"Nathaniel." Her voice is a whisper, edged with disbelief and warning.

He steps into view, his silhouette cutting through the pale morning light. His gaze never wavers, locking onto hers with quiet intensity.

"You will listen to me," he says firmly.

Her breath hitches, but she steels herself, turning swiftly toward the door.

He moves before she can escape, blocking her path with practiced ease. His presence is not threatening, but it is undeniable, unrelenting.

"I have no interest in playing games, Evangeline." His voice is low, steady. "I know something is wrong."

She lifts her chin, her expression a perfect mask of indifference. "You are mistaken."

He exhales sharply.

"I saw your wrist."

For the first time, her composure falters. It is the barest flicker, a shadow passing through her gaze, but Nathaniel seizes upon it.

Silence stretches between them, thick with unspoken truths.

"Tell me," he urges. "Tell me what he's done to you."

Evangeline closes her eyes briefly, a breath shuddering through her. Then she steps back—not in fear, but in dismissal.

"There is nothing to tell."

Nathaniel's hands curl into fists at his sides. He knows she is lying. He knows she is afraid.

And he knows he will not stop until he finds the truth.

Nathaniel's breath is slow, measured, but inside, he is anything but calm. The weight of Evangeline's dismissal hangs in the air between them, thick and suffocating. His heart pounds against his ribs, fury warring with desperation.

She is lying to him. And she knows that he knows.

"Evangeline," he says, his voice quieter now, but no less intense. "I saw it."

She does not move, but he catches the way her fingers twitch at her sides, as if resisting the urge to pull her sleeves further down.

"I don't know what you think you saw," she replies, turning her face away.

Nathaniel takes a step closer, forcing her to meet his gaze. "Then look me in the eye and tell me it was nothing."

Evangeline's throat bobs as she swallows, but her expression remains impassive. "I do not owe you any explanations."

His jaw clenches. "After everything, you still think you can lie to me?"

She exhales sharply. "You are in NO position to lecture ME on affairs of honesty. You think you know everything, Nathaniel? That you can just storm back into my life and demand answers as if you have the right?" Her voice rises slightly, the first crack in her armor. "You gave up that right a long time ago."

He flinches, but only for a second.

"This is not about us." His voice is quiet but firm. "This is about you."

She lets out a short, bitter laugh, shaking her head. "There is no 'me' and 'you,' Nathaniel. You are chasing ghosts."

His hands curl into fists at his sides. He could walk away. Let her bury herself in these lies, let her continue pretending. But the image of that mark on her wrist burns in his mind, an accusation, a cry for help she refuses to voice.

"You flinched," he says, softer now, almost hesitant. "When I touched you."

That is when she truly stills. Her fingers tighten around the folds of her skirt, her breathing shallow. For a moment, just a moment, he thinks she might say something. That she might finally give him the truth.

But instead, she steps back, further into the shadows of the greenhouse.

"You need to leave."

Nathaniel shakes his head. "Not until you tell me—"

"There is nothing to tell," she interrupts, her voice devoid of all emotion.

The door to the greenhouse is still open, the morning light beginning to break through the glass panes, casting streaks of gold against the damp earth. Evangeline stands in that light, but she is pale, distant, unreachable.

Nathaniel watches her for a long moment, his chest rising

and falling with the effort of restraining everything he wants to say, everything he wants to do.

But he knows better than to push her. Not yet.

Instead, he exhales, slow and even. "Fine," he murmurs. "I'll go."

He moves toward the door, pausing only once. "But this isn't over, Evangeline."

She says nothing, her expression unreadable.

Nathaniel steps outside, letting the door close behind him. The cool air does nothing to settle the fire inside him.

He had given her a chance to tell him the truth.

Now, he would find it himself.

Nathaniel had meant to walk away. Had told himself to leave her be.

But something—something in the way she stood there, rigid and hollow, her hands trembling ever so slightly at her sides—made him hesitate.

He turns back, his gaze locking onto her, searching, pleading. He steps forward, slow and careful, as if approaching a wounded creature.

"Evangeline..."

Her breath catches. She does not look at him, does not move, but he sees the way her fingers curl around the delicate fabric of her shawl. As if anchoring herself.

He reaches for her, fingers grazing her wrist. A light touch, barely there.

She inhales sharply—not in fear, but in something far worse: longing. The moment stretches, taut and fragile. He can feel the warmth of her skin beneath his fingertips, the rapid beat of her pulse.

"You can lie to yourself," he murmurs, voice hushed and reverent, "but not to me."

For a second, she falters.

Her lips part, her eyes darken, and she leans in—just a fraction. The barrier between them wavers, thin as glass. He can almost see the woman he once knew, the woman who had once looked at him as though he was the only man in the world.

Then—

A breath. A realization.

She rips herself away from him as though burned, wrapping her arms tightly around her middle, as if to contain whatever war rages inside her. Her entire body is trembling, but her voice—when she speaks—is hollow, lifeless.

"This conversation is over."

Nathaniel lets her go. He knows he cannot force the truth from her lips. But as she turns from him, as she lifts her shawl around herself with hands that will not steady—he knows.

The crack has begun.

Chapter Four

The study is dimly lit, the only source of light the dying embers in the hearth, casting restless shadows against the mahogany-panelled walls. Nathaniel sits in the leather armchair, the weight of the night pressing heavy on his shoulders. Before him, a half-empty glass of brandy rests on the desk, untouched for some time now. His fingers toy with the rim, but he does not drink.

He stares into the fire, yet all he sees is her.

Evangeline's trembling hands. The way she recoiled from his touch. The way she wrapped her shawl around herself as though it could shield her from him—from the truth she refused to speak.

But beyond that moment, another memory stirs, clawing its way to the surface, bringing with it the weight of his greatest mistake.

The scent of jasmine lingers in the air, a cruel trick of memory. It had been there that night too…

The night he lost her forever.

It had started with laughter—low, indulgent, wrapped in the heady haze of brandy and candlelight. The whiff of expensive perfume, the silken feel of fingertips grazing over his wrist.

But none of it had mattered. He barely remembered the woman's name.

What he did remember—what had been burned into him—was the moment he woke to the wrong person beside him.

The slow, sickening clarity. The unfamiliar scent of roses and something too sweet. Silk sheets tangled with his own, the heat of another body still lingering.

Then—

The door creaked open.

A sharp inhale.

Evangeline.

Nathaniel grips the arms of his chair, knuckles white, as the memory unfurls like a nightmare that refuses to fade.

His head had been pounding, the weight of sleep and brandy still fogging his thoughts. He had turned, confusion tightening his chest, only to find Madame Vivienne beside him—her golden hair spilling over his pillow, her lips curled into a lazy, knowing smile.

No. No, this isn't—

Then the sound of fabric rustling, soft but deafening in the stunned silence.

The door stood wide open.

Evangeline.

She was bathed in the flickering candlelight, still in her evening gown, dark curls tumbling over her shoulders. But her eyes—

Her eyes were what undid him.

Wide. Hollow. A storm gathered behind them, but she said nothing. No accusations, no fury, no heartbreak spilling from her lips. Just silence, chilling and absolute.

"Evangeline," he had gasped, his throat raw, his hands reaching for her, but she was already stepping back. A single, hesitant step—

Then another.

Then she was gone.

Nathaniel had stumbled from the bed, nearly falling in his frantic desperation. He had shouted her name, chased her into the corridor, his vision swimming, his chest tightening with panic. But she never once turned back.

His bare feet had slapped against the cold stone floor, his breath coming in ragged gasps. The grand staircase loomed ahead, and for a moment, just a moment, he thought he could reach her. Thought he could stop her.

But by the time he reached the foyer, the great doors had already slammed shut.

She was gone.

And he had never stopped paying for it.

Nathaniel had no excuse. No grand conspiracy to pin his actions on. No elaborate scheme that could absolve him of blame.

He had been drunk. He had been reckless. And he had destroyed the only woman he had ever loved.

He remembers how he had stood there, staring at the door long after she left, unable to move, unable to accept what he had done. His breath had come in sharp, uneven gasps, the heavy silence of the chamber pressing in on him. The scent of jasmine still lingered in the air, mocking him, a cruel reminder of what he had just lost.

The guilt had settled like lead in his chest, thick and suffocating. It had been all-consuming, swallowing him whole. He had wanted to run after her, to fall at her feet and beg her to listen—to believe that there had to be some way to fix what he had broken.

But what words could possibly make this right?

Nathaniel had replayed it in his mind a thousand times over the years, searching for the moment where he might have done something differently, grasping for an alternate path that did not lead to ruin. But there was none. There was only this —his regret, and the empty ache where Evangeline had once been.

A year later, the regret still lingers. A spectre that follows him, never quite fading.

Nathaniel had avoided Madame Vivienne's establishment for a long time. He had walked past it more times than he cared to count, each step dragging with the weight of memories he wished he could erase. But now, with his resolve set like iron, he forces himself to return.

The familiar scent of perfume and wine clings to the air as he steps inside, the dim lighting casting long, shifting shadows against the rich velvet drapery. The hum of laughter and whispered secrets fills the space, but it is all just background noise to him. His focus narrows on one woman alone.

Madame Vivienne lounges against a settee, her gown of deep burgundy pooling around her in decadent folds. She lifts her glass as he approaches, her painted lips curving into a knowing smile.

"To what do I owe this pleasure, my lord?" she purrs, swirling her wine lazily, her eyes sharp with amusement.

She is surprised to see him. It is in the way her fingers pause on the glass stem, the slight raise of a brow. For a fleeting moment, she thought he had come for pleasure, for comfort. But then—she sees the look in his eyes. Cold. Hardened. She realises *this* visit is different.

"You're not here for company?" she muses, smirking. "A shame. I always thought you might return, after all."

Nathaniel does not respond. His stare is unrelenting.

Her smirk falters. "Ah," she hums, taking another sip of wine, "so what is it then?"

"I need answers."

She tilts her head, considering him. Then she smirks again, though it does not reach her eyes. "Regret doesn't suit you, Nathaniel."

His jaw tightens. "Spare me the performance. Did Evangeline ever—"

Vivienne hums softly, dragging her nail along the rim of her glass. "Why would she? She saw what she needed to see."

A bitter weight settles in his stomach. He already knew the answer, but hearing it aloud twists the knife deeper.

Evangeline had never doubted what she saw. Because he had given her no reason to.

But something about this had *never* sat right with him. The way she had *walked in* on him and Vivienne—when she was meant to be away. The way the news had spread like wildfire, how within mere hours, every drawing room in London was alight with scandal. How the whispers had hounded her, louder and crueler than they had ever been to him. How her reputation had *collapsed*, forcing her into hiding for nearly a year.

And now? A year later, she was suddenly *engaged to a duke*?

Nathaniel's hands curl into fists. He had been too blind—too *drowning* in his own shame—to question it before. But now, standing before Vivienne, looking into her eyes, he *sees* it.

She knows something.

"How much?" His voice is quiet, but it slices through the space between them like a blade.

Vivienne does not feign ignorance. She takes a slow sip of her wine, holding his gaze over the rim of her glass. "Five thousand pounds."

Nathaniel's stomach turns. *A fortune.*

"Ashford?" he asks, his voice flat, though rage burns beneath the surface.

Vivienne's lips curve, but there is no mirth in her expression. "I do not name my benefactors. But let us say... a *duke* found it in his best interest that you and Lady Evangeline be parted. That she be ruined in such a way that she had little choice but to accept a carefully placed offer of salvation."

Nathaniel barely hears the rest. Blood pounds in his ears,

his vision tunnelling. *A duke. Ashford.* The pieces align, and suddenly, the past does not look like a mistake.

It looks like a *trap*.

Vivienne watches him carefully, her smirk thinning. Then, in a slow, deliberate movement, she stands and approaches. Her perfume—thick and heady—wraps around him as she presses a hand to his chest, tilting her head.

"You've had it so hard," she whispers, her fingers trailing lightly over his coat. "So much suffering. So much pain."

She leans in, her lips grazing just beneath his jaw. "Why not let me ease it? Just for a few hours."

Temptation is a living thing. It coils around him, burrows deep. He has the last year steeped in regret, in guilt, in longing. She is soft, offering relief, escape.

Her lips brush his skin, warm and inviting, and for a moment, he lets his eyes close. A sharp breath escapes him, his body taut with something unspoken. She smells of jasmine and wine, of silk sheets and forgotten sins.

Just once. Just for tonight.

His fingers twitch at his sides. His throat goes dry. *It would be easy.*

For one fractured second, he almost caves.

His hands twitch, his restraint paper-thin—until Ashford's name slices through the haze like a blade.

Then—

His hand snaps up, gripping her wrist—firm, but not cruel. He pulls back, meeting her gaze with ice-cold determination.

"Who was it?" His voice is steel, cutting through the intimacy of the moment. "Who paid you off?"

Vivienne's eyes flicker to the door, as if expecting someone to be standing there, listening. When she speaks again, her voice drops to a whisper, barely audible above the crackling of the fire.

Vivienne searches his face, something guarded flashing

through her eyes. Then she exhales, stepping away, shaking her head. "You should let this go, Nathaniel."

He watches her, unblinking.

"Ashford," he says, voice deathly quiet.

She hesitates—just a flicker. But that's all he needs.

Her lips part, then press together. "You don't understand," she says quietly. "Ashford... he's not like the others. He's taken girls before. A few of mine." Her throat bobs as she swallows, lowering her voice further. "They always came back with bruises. But he's a duke, and they're just whores. Who is the public going to believe?"

Nathaniel's fists tighten at his sides. "And you let it continue?"

She swallows hard, her bravado cracking. "There's not a lot of opportunities for girls like us, Nathaniel. We've made the best of a bad situation. But you... you could burn it all down without realising."

Vivienne bristles, her expression turning defensive. "Do you think there's a choice in this, my lord? Do you think I haven't tried? That I haven't done what I can to protect them? There are not many opportunities for women like us, and I have a business to run. If I cross the wrong man, there will be no one left to protect my girls."

He turns to walk away, angry and disappointed but Vivienne grips his wrist suddenly, her nails pressing into his skin. "It's not that simple," she hisses. "You confront him openly, and you'll sign my death warrant. Not just mine—*theirs*."

Her voice is sharp, her eyes flinty with defiance, but there is truth in them. Fear.

Nathaniel exhales through his nose, his rage simmering just beneath the surface. He still doesn't like her, still doesn't trust her. But he understands now.

He steps closer, voice lowering. "No harm shall befall you," he murmurs, "at least not from me."

"You think this is about Evangeline?" Vivienne's voice

drops lower. "She's not the first. And if you're not careful, she won't be the last."

Silence.

Vivienne searches his face for a long moment, then nods once, almost imperceptibly. "Be careful, Nathaniel," she whispers. "You don't know what you're dealing with."

He doesn't reply.

He turns sharply on his heel, his purpose set, his fury burning hot.

He leaves her premises with a new fire in his chest—and more reason than ever to suspect Ashford.

Nathaniel steps out into the cold night, the weight of his conversation with Madame Vivienne pressing against his chest like a vice. The air is crisp, biting against his skin, but he barely feels it. His thoughts are consumed by a single, unshakable truth.

He had lost Evangeline by his own doing, he does not shroud his actions in justifications, but if Ashford had harmed her—if there was even the smallest truth to the unease he had seen in her eyes—he would not sit idly by. No force in heaven or hell would stop him from uncovering the truth.

He strides through the cobbled streets with renewed purpose, each step harder than the last. The dim glow of gas lamps flickers along the pavement, their golden light casting elongated shadows. The city around him is alive with muted laughter, the hum of distant carriage wheels, the sound of lives continuing as if nothing in the world had changed.

But for Nathaniel, everything had.

His jaw tightens as he straightens his coat, his fingers curling into fists at his sides. He has never been a patient man. And this—

This is war.

Regret had once made him weak, had once shackled him in self-loathing. No longer. This time, he would not fail her.

This time, he would fight for her, even if she refused to ask for his help.

The truth was out there, buried beneath layers of deception, hidden in the shadows of Ashford's pristine reputation. Nathaniel would find it.

He would burn through every lie until he reached the core of it.

A slow exhale leaves his lips, and as he loosens his grip, the brandy glass slips from his fingers, shattering against the cobblestones.

He does not flinch. Does not even spare it a glance.

Nathaniel exhales, slow and even, but the fire inside him has already caught. *Ashford thought this was over.*

He flexes his fingers, the memory of Vivienne's fear searing into his bones.

He was wrong.

Let the game begin.

Chapter Five

The evening air is thick with the scent of damp stone and rain. The streets glisten under the dim glow of street lanterns, puddles forming along the cobblestone paths. Water trickles through the cracks in the pavement, the distant murmur of carriage wheels mingling with the soft patter of rain.

Evangeline moves swiftly, her cloak wrapped tightly around her, shielding herself from the evening chill. The weight of the night's festivities lingers behind her—the laughter, the music, the suffocating presence of *him*. She needs air, space.

She turns down a quiet alleyway beside the grand hall, her steps light, purposeful. She should not be out here alone, but the thought of remaining inside—trapped in that gilded cage, surrounded by whispered judgments—suffocates her.

Nathaniel sees her before she sees him.

He hadn't planned on this—hadn't expected to find her here, slipping away like a ghost into the night. His blood hums with purpose, still raw from his meeting with Vivienne, his mind clouded with unanswered questions. But all of that fades as the dim lantern light catches the curve of her face beneath her hood, her figure wrapped in shadows and silk.

Then—

A gust of wind rushes between them, carrying the scent of rain and jasmine. It's enough to stir something deep in his chest, something sharp and unrelenting.

He steps into her path.

"Evangeline."

She halts abruptly, her grip tightening around her cloak. Rain drips from the edges of her hood as she lifts her gaze, eyes flashing in the dim light.

"What do you want?" Her voice is cool, edged with something *else*—something she refuses to name.

Nathaniel's pulse thrums. He had planned to find her —*speak* to her—but not like this. Not in the rain, with the world closing in around them, the silence stretching like a blade between them.

"Please," he says, his voice raw, pleading. "Just hear me out."

Her expression does not soften. "We have nothing to say to each other." She steps sideways, intending to pass him, but he moves with her, blocking her escape.

"I know I have no right to ask this of you," he murmurs, rain sliding down his temples, soaking into his coat. "But you deserve to know the truth."

Evangeline laughs, a cold, hollow sound. "The truth?" She shakes her head, the motion sharp. "The truth is that I walked into your chambers and saw you with another woman. There is nothing else I need to know."

Nathaniel flinches, but he does not back down. "I was drunk," he admits, his voice tight with self-loathing. "And it was a mistake I have paid for every single day since."

Her jaw tightens. She does not want to hear this. She does not want to *remember*.

"I spoke to Vivienne," he says, and this time, he sees it—

the flicker of something in her gaze. A crack in the ice. "She was *paid* to be there that night."

She stiffens.

"I know what I did," he continues, stepping closer, his voice dropping to something rough, something desperate. "But tell me—don't you think it's strange? How quickly it happened? How *perfectly timed* your arrival was?"

Silence stretches between them, thick with ghosts. A single raindrop slides down the curve of her cheek, but she does not move.

Evangeline tries to be logical, to weigh reason against the past, but the wounds of that night still linger, raw and unrelenting. In this moment, there is no room for reason—only the crushing weight of betrayal.

"A mistake?" she echoes at last, her voice sharp as glass. Her expression remains unreadable, but he sees the way her fingers dig into the folds of her cloak, sees the way her shoulders rise, tense with something unspoken. "You once told me I was the only thing you ever wanted. Was that before or after you took another woman to bed?"

Nathaniel breathes deeply, willing himself to remain steady, to push through the rage, the regret. "You were *always* the only thing I ever wanted."

A fresh gust of wind sweeps through the alley, sending a shiver down Evangeline's spine. But she does not look away.

"Then why did you destroy me?"

Nathaniel flinches—because it is not anger in her voice now.

It is pain.

And that is so much worse.

Nathaniel takes a step closer, rain soaking into his coat, his expression open, desperate. The night air is thick with the weight of words left unsaid, the scent of rain and stone mingling between them.

"Evangeline, if I could take it back, I would. But I can't. All I can do is tell you the truth now."

She turns her head away, but he catches the way her fingers tremble at her sides, betraying the steel in her voice. She does not want to listen. She does not want to be here. And yet, she has not left.

"Just talk to me," he presses. "That's all I ask. Five minutes. And if, after that, you still want me to leave, I will."

A gust of wind rushes between them, carrying the scent of jasmine, of memories that neither of them dares to acknowledge.

Evangeline scoffs, shaking her head. "Why? What could you possibly say that would change anything?"

Nathaniel exhales, his voice low, aching. "Because I need to know if there's still a chance. If I can still fight for you. I know I failed you once, but I will not fail you again. I know what he is, Evangeline. I know what he's done. And I know I can be better for you—because I already am.

I will not stand by while you suffer under him. You think I don't see it? The way you flinch when he touches you, the way your smile never quite reaches your eyes anymore? You may not want to admit it, but I know. And I swear to you, on everything I am, I will prove I am not the man I was that night. I will fight for you—even if you won't let me."

Evangeline's breath catches, her fingers tightening at her sides. For a moment, something flashes in her eyes—pain, hesitation, a deep-seated yearning she has spent too long denying. But just as quickly, her expression hardens again.

"It's too late," she whispers. "Too much has happened."

She turns sharply, intending to walk past him, but Nathaniel moves swiftly, stepping in front of her. The rain clings to his hair, his coat, but he does not yield.

"Let me pass," she commands, her voice sharp.

"No," he says simply.

Her lips press together. "Nathaniel—"

For the briefest moment, something flickers in her eyes—a crack in the armour she has so carefully built. It's gone in an instant, buried beneath practiced indifference, but Nathaniel sees it. A hesitation. A breath that falters. Her fingers twitch at her sides, curling into the fabric of her cloak as if to steady herself. *Does he hurt you?* The question burns on his tongue, but before he can give it life, she steels herself. Her chin lifts, her expression smoothing into something cold, untouchable. "You know nothing about my life, Nathaniel," she says, but her voice is just a little too even, her composure just a little too perfect.

"Please, just hear me out," he pleads, his voice rough with emotion. "If after this, you still wish to walk away, I won't stop you. But not like this. Not without knowing the truth.". I know I failed you once, but I will not fail you again. I know what he is, Evangeline. I know what he's done. And I know I can be better for you—because I already am.

Hatred coils in Nathaniel's chest, dark and insidious, growing sharper with every moment Evangeline refuses to speak the truth. He can see it—the flicker of fear, the way she almost gives something away before forcing herself to retreat behind that impenetrable mask. And it infuriates him. Not at her, never at her, but at *him*. At Ashford. That smug, well-bred bastard who thought he could own her, control her, break her. Nathaniel grits his teeth, his hands curling into fists at his sides. He had once been a fool, blind to the games of men like Ashford. But not anymore. Now, he sees it for what it is—a battle. And Nathaniel Sinclair has never been one to walk away from a fight.

A sharp breath.

She does not answer. Not immediately. But she does not walk away either. Her silence speaks of an internal war, one she has fought for far too long.

Rain trickles from the edge of his jaw, the quiet patter of droplets filling the space between them. She stands before him, cloaked in defiance, but he can see past it—to the part of her that still remembers, that still feels.

A deafening Silence. It stretches between them, an unspoken challenge, a question neither of them dares to voice.

For the first time, she does not lash out. She does not leave.

Her hands tighten in the folds of her cloak, as if trying to hold herself together. The wind howls through the narrow alley, but neither of them moves. Nathaniel watches the tension in her shoulders, the rise and fall of her breath, the war behind her eyes.

He is different now. She knows it. But knowing and believing are not the same thing.

The rain seeps through the fabric of her cloak, cold against her skin, but it is nothing compared to the storm within. She had once trusted him without question, had once thought his love was an unshakable force—until the night she found him with another. That night had broken something in her, something she had never managed to repair. And yet, as he speaks, as his voice—that voice—wraps around her like a whisper from the past, her body betrays her. The way her breath hitches, the way her pulse stirs in defiance of the walls she has built—it makes her furious. She wants to feel nothing. Wants to let his words fall into the void where her love for him used to be. But the past refuses to be buried so easily.

"You don't have to trust me. But trust yourself. Trust that you know the truth when you hear it."

Finally, Evangeline exhales, shaking her head as if she hates herself for even considering it.

"Five minutes."

Nathaniel releases a breath he hadn't realised he was holding. Relief washes through him, but he does not let it show. He knows this battle is far from over.

He nods, voice quiet. "Thank you."

The storm has not passed.

But the first crack has formed.

Chapter Six

Nathaniel's breath is unsteady, the rain sliding down his face like the guilt that has haunted him for a year. The weight of regret presses against his ribs, heavier than the sodden fabric clinging to his skin. He has played this moment over and over in his mind—what he would say, how he would say it—but nothing prepared him for how she looks at him now. Cold. Detached. Like he is nothing but a spectre of a past she has long since buried.

"I don't deserve your forgiveness," he murmurs. "I know that. But you need to understand—I never meant to ruin you. I never meant for my mistake to stain your name."

Evangeline's lips press into a thin line. "It doesn't matter what you meant. It happened. And I paid for it."

His chest tightens. "I know."

Silence stretches between them, only the rain filling the space where words fail. It weaves between them, settling in the cracks of their past, an ever-present reminder of all that was lost. It seeps through his coat, his shirt—cold against his skin, but not as cold as the chasm that now exists between them. She is close enough that he could reach out and touch her, yet she might as well be an ocean away.

He swallows hard, forcing the words past the tightness in his throat. "Do you love him?" His voice is hoarse, barely audible over the storm, but he knows she hears him. He sees it in the way her shoulders stiffen, in the way her breath falters for just a moment too long.

A flicker of something in her eyes—hesitation.

That's all the confirmation he needs.

Nathaniel's jaw clenches. The words he has wanted to ignore now press against his ribs, demanding to be spoken.

"Does he hurt you?" Nathaniel's voice is barely more than a breath, yet it cuts through the space between them like a blade.

A memory coils around her, suffocating. The opera house—candlelight flickering against polished marble, the scent of perfume and power hanging in the air. Ashford's fingers had curled around her wrist, deceptively light, his grip like silk over steel. His lips had ghosted over her ear, his voice as smooth as velvet, laced with quiet menace.

"You are mine, Evangeline. No one will take you from me. And if they try..."

His smile had been slow, deliberate—a promise, not a threat. And it still haunts her.

She swallows hard. "This isn't about you, Nathaniel."

But her voice wavers, and they both hear it.

She opens her mouth to force another lie, to stitch together something convincing—but the words won't come.

She is frozen, her throat tightening, her silence a confession in itself.

"Evangeline—" he steps forward, but she holds up a hand. "Why do you care?" she demands, her voice trembling.

"Because I do!" The words rip from him, raw and fierce. "Because I have spent every night since losing you wishing I could take it back. Wishing it had been me waiting for you at the altar. Wishing I had been the man who could make you happy."

The rain drips from her lashes, but it does nothing to hide the anger, the heartbreak, the longing warring in her eyes. She shakes her head, as if willing herself not to listen, not to feel, but he sees it—the hesitation, the way she falters just for a breath of a second.

"I know what I did," he continues, his voice rough. "I know I destroyed the life we should have had. But you think I don't see it? How much you've changed? How much he's changed you?"

Evangeline flinches—just barely, but he catches it.

A sharp inhale. The briefest shift of her gaze.

And then she turns away.

Nathaniel doesn't hesitate. He moves before she can step further into the night, his fingers brushing her wrist. Not gripping, not forcing—just a touch.

She goes rigid.

"Tell me the truth," he pleads. "Not for me. For you."

For a moment, the rain is the only sound between them, falling in heavy sheets against the cobblestone. Then, softly—

"It doesn't matter," she whispers, and the words cut him deeper than any blade ever could.

Nathaniel exhales sharply, his jaw tightening. "I know I don't deserve you. But tell me—does he make you feel alive, Evangeline? Or are you just surviving?"

Her breath catches. A flicker of something—guilt, longing, fear—crosses her face, gone before he can grasp it.

Because it does.

It matters more than anything.

And he will not stop until she admits it.

Evangeline's chest rises and falls with uneven breaths, though whether it's from anger or something far more dangerous, she refuses to acknowledge. The rain clings to her lashes, her cloak heavy with water, yet she feels no cold—only the searing heat of Nathaniel's presence, too close, too relentless.

"You don't get to say that now," she spits, her voice sharp

as a blade. "You don't get to act as if you still have a right to me after what you did."

Nathaniel exhales, his breath unsteady, his eyes burning with something raw. "I know I don't." His voice is hoarse, barely audible over the storm. "But that doesn't change the fact that no man, not even Ashford, will ever love you as much as I do."

"Love?" she laughs, but there is no joy in it, only bitter, frayed edges. "Love doesn't betray. Love doesn't destroy. Love doesn't—"

"Love doesn't give up," Nathaniel cuts her off, his voice a whisper, aching, desperate. "And I never have."

Evangeline's fingers twitch at her sides, curling into fists. "You should have," she says, but it lacks the conviction she wishes it had. She steps back, but he follows, his presence unwavering, his intensity a force that shakes something loose inside her.

"I love you, Evangeline. I never stopped. I never will."

The words slice through the storm, through the years of pain, settling deep in the spaces between them. He is standing so close now, his breath mingling with hers, the rain soaking through both of them, but neither notices.

Evangeline forces herself to hold his gaze, to ignore the way her pulse hammers against her ribs, the way the sound of his voice wraps around her like something familiar, something safe.

"You are lying to yourself," he murmurs, his gaze searching hers. "I see it in your eyes."

She glares at him, jaw tight, her entire body rigid with the war raging inside her. "I hate you," she bites out, each word carefully measured, carefully aimed.

Nathaniel exhales sharply, but he does not flinch. He looks at her as if seeing something beyond the anger, beyond the sharp words meant to wound him.

"No, you don't," he murmurs, his voice steady, certain.

The space between them is suffocating.

The rain drips from her lashes. She opens her mouth—maybe to deny it, maybe to lash out, maybe to say something that will shatter what remains between them.

But no words come.

Her fingers curl into the fabric of her dress, gripping tight—too tight.

Because if she speaks, she will have to lie.

And she is so very tired of lying.

The rain has soaked them through, yet neither of them moves away. The air between them is thick, charged with something neither of them dares to name. Evangeline's breath is uneven, her pulse hammering in her ears, drowning out every rational thought. She should run. She should push him away, say something cruel, something final.

But she doesn't.

Nathaniel looks at her as though this is his last chance, his last moment before the world rips them apart again. He takes a slow step forward, closing the distance inch by inch, his voice low and insistent. "Are you going to deny what we have? Deny what we are?"

Evangeline stiffens, a bitter laugh escaping her lips. "You only want me because I'm with another. Men only want what they can't have."

Nathaniel shakes his head, the rain streaming down his face. "No. I want you because you're *you*. Because I have loved you every second of every day, even when you hated me. Even when I hated myself."

She swallows hard, but doesn't move away. He inches closer still, his gaze flicking down to her lips, his breath mingling with hers. His hands twitch, aching to reach for her. And she knows—knows that this is not some fleeting desire. This is love, raw and unyielding. His chest rises and falls in sharp, uneven breaths, his fingers twitching at his sides like he's holding himself back, as if this is a battle between restraint and need.

"Nathaniel, I—"

Her voice falters. She doesn't know what she meant to say —only that it wouldn't have been the truth.

Nathaniel stills. His breath is uneven, his forehead pressing against hers as though grounding himself in the feel of her. His thumb brushes against her cheekbone, soft, reverent, as if committing her to memory—like he fears she will slip through his fingers once more.

"I lost you," he whispers, the words nearly breaking.

Evangeline freezes.

For a moment, she sees it—not the rogue, not the man who ruined her, but the boy who had once held her in a sunlit garden and promised forever. The boy who had kissed her with laughter on his lips, who had spoken of futures built side by side. The boy she had loved with everything in her heart.

But that boy is gone.

And she cannot afford to believe in ghosts.

So she kisses him before he can say anything else—before he can break her all over again.

His lips crash against hers, hot, desperate, devouring. A shuddering gasp escapes her, but she doesn't pull away. Her hands fist against his soaked coat, not pushing him away, not pulling him closer—just holding on. Holding on to the storm raging inside her, to the battle between her heart and her fury.

Holding on—because she doesn't know how to let go.

Nathaniel groans against her mouth, his hands coming up to cradle her face, his touch reverent yet unrelenting. He deepens the kiss, and that's when something inside her shatters.

A trembling breath. A hand sliding up his chest, fingers curling into the fabric of his shirt—

No. This cannot happen.

Ashford will know. He always knows.

A flash of bruises, hidden beneath lace. A voice at her ear —smooth as silk, sharp as steel.

"If you make me look a fool, Evangeline, I will remind you what happens to disobedient women."

Nathaniel's hands tremble at her waist, his breath warm against her skin. He is waiting—for permission, for rejection, for anything.

And yet... she gives him neither.

She should not crave him like this.

She should not tremble beneath his hands like a woman untouched, a woman waiting to be claimed.

She should despise him.

But she doesn't.

His grip tightens on her waist, not enough to hurt, but enough for her to feel the raw, trembling restraint in him.

He is close to breaking. She can feel it in the way his breath shudders against her lips, in the way his fingers clutch at her as though she is the only thing tethering him to this world.

And maybe... she is.

Then, finally—she lets herself feel it.

All the anger, all the pain, all the years lost between them—

It collides in that kiss.

She should stop this. She should push him away.

But, God help her—she doesn't want to.

He had kissed her as though his life depended on it, and now she was slipping through his fingers once more. The taste of desperation and longing, of rain and regret, still lingered on her lips. The heat of him had seeped through her frozen skin, awakening something inside her she thought had long since withered. The way he had held her—firm, as if terrified she would slip through his fingers again—undid her more than she was willing to admit.

For the first time in so long, she feels... *safe*.

Not trapped, not helpless, not waiting for the next sharp-edged command to fall from Ashford's lips.

She is warm. She is wanted.

She is... *home*.

The realization slams into her like a blade between the ribs.

Her breath shudders.

Nathaniel's fingers twitch against her skin, as though he can sense it too.

And that is why she cannot stay.

Then suddenly, she rips herself away, gasping, her chest heaving as though she has just surfaced from drowning.

Nathaniel stares at her, his expression raw, exposed. His breath is ragged, his lips swollen from the force of it, but he does not reach for her again.

"Tell me to leave," he breathes. "Tell me you feel nothing, and I swear, I will never come near you again."

Evangeline stares at him, her heart pounding against her ribs, her fingers still curled into the damp fabric of her dress.

She should tell him to go.

It would be so easy—three words, and this would be over.

But she doesn't answer.

Because she can't.

Chapter Seven

The door slams shut behind them, the sound muffled by the storm still raging outside. Rain drips from their clothes, pooling onto the marble floor, but neither of them cares. The moment stretches between them, thick with heat and unspoken words, their breaths shallow and unsteady.

Evangeline shivers, though not from the cold. The soaked fabric of her dress clings to her curves, heavy against her skin. Nathaniel stands before her, his chest rising and falling in sharp, uneven breaths, his gaze dark with something raw, something undeniable.

Then he moves.

His hands find her waist, her hips, the laces of her corset as though he has no control, no restraint left in him. Her back meets the wall, the cold surface a sharp contrast to the searing heat of him pressing against her.

There are no more words. No more denials. Only the crackling intensity between them, a fire long buried beneath resentment and regret.

Their mouths crash together, desperate, punishing, as if

trying to erase the years of distance between them, as if trying to drown out the pain with something just as consuming. Her fingers tangle into his damp hair, tugging, her nails scraping against his scalp. He groans into her mouth, deep and aching, his hands everywhere, mapping the shape of her as if trying to memorise her all over again.

Nathaniel's jacket hits the floor. Then his cravat. Then the rest of the layers between them, peeled away with the same frantic urgency as their kisses.

Evangeline trembles. Not from the storm, not from the chill, but from the sheer recklessness of this moment.

"Tell me to stop," Nathaniel rasps against her throat, his breath scorching against her skin.

She should. She doesn't.

Instead, her hands push at his shirt, dragging it over his shoulders, her nails scraping against his bare chest. He shudders beneath her touch, a sound escaping his lips that is more prayer than pleasure.

His forehead presses against hers, his breath warm, unsteady. His hands tremble slightly as they ghost over her ribs, her waist, lower. Not from hesitation—but because he knows the weight of this moment.

His fingers skim along the delicate curve of her spine, dipping lower, tracing the wet fabric that clings to her thighs. She gasps, and he swallows the sound, his lips finding the sensitive skin just below her ear, his breath sending a tremor through her. He is worshipping her with touch alone, memorising the shape of her with reverent, aching slowness.

"You still feel this," he whispers, his voice low, reverent, filled with something that terrifies her.

She does. God, she does.

Her body is betraying her, responding to him in ways she wishes it wouldn't, in ways she can't ignore. Her heart pounds violently against her ribs, her breath shuddering as he pulls her closer, until there is nothing between them but heat, history, and years of longing left unsaid.

She exhales shakily, her fingers threading through his hair, nails scraping lightly against his scalp as his lips trail down the column of her throat. Her head tilts back against the wall, exposing herself to him, to his touch, to the way he unravels her without effort.

And for the first time in a very long time—

Evangeline doesn't want to fight it.

Nathaniel has never known fear like this—not even in the moment he lost her all those years ago. That had been pain. A clean, searing wound. This? This is something else entirely. A slow, merciless unraveling, as if she is peeling him apart layer by layer and deciding, with each passing second, whether she will choose to break him or save him.

She is beneath him now, breathless, her skin damp with rain and heat, her fingers tangled in his hair. Yet even now, even as she allows him this, she is holding something back. He can feel it—the resistance, the unspoken words, the walls she refuses to let crumble.

His hands shake as they worship her body, tracing every dip and curve as though praying at an altar. He kisses her—slow and deep, then frantic, then reverent again, as though she is something holy and untouchable, yet here she is, in his arms.

But still, she does not give him what he wants most.

The words. The acknowledgment. The surrender.

He presses his forehead to hers, breath ragged. "Look at me," he murmurs, tilting her chin up with trembling fingers. "Evangeline."

She hesitates—because she knows if she does, she will break.

"Tell me this means nothing to you," he whispers, his lips brushing the corner of her mouth. "Tell me, and I will stop. I will let you go."

Her breath hitches, but still, she says nothing.

"I love you." His voice is hoarse, raw with something unbreakable. "I have never stopped. And I never will."

Her lashes flutter, her hands pressing flat against his chest as if to push him away—but her fingers curl, betraying her. Betraying them both.

"Nathaniel," she exhales, his name half a whisper, half a plea.

It destroys him.

His lips crash into hers again, desperate, devoted, his hands gripping her as though she is the only thing anchoring him to this world. He pours everything into that kiss—all his regret, his love, his promises. And for a moment, she gives in.

She should stop this. She should push him away, remind him of all the ways he ruined her, all the nights she spent alone, humiliated, broken. But as his fingers trace along her jaw, as his lips brush against hers, she feels the war inside her unraveling. How could she still want him? How could she still ache for him?

Her fingers clutch at his shoulders, pulling him closer, not away, her nails dragging across his skin, leaving marks that are neither of pain nor protest. His hands roam, hungry and seeking, sliding down the curve of her back, pressing her body flush against his, until there is nothing left between them but heat and need.

She has spent a year rebuilding the walls he shattered. But with every breath he takes, with every whispered plea, those walls begin to crumble. And she is terrified of what will be left if she lets them fall completely.

A gasp escapes her lips as he trails kisses down her throat, his mouth worshiping the skin that has haunted him in dreams. Her head tilts back, her body arching instinctively, surrendering to the way his hands grasp her hips, lifting, pressing, claiming.

Her walls falter just for a breath, just for a moment—but it is enough.

But then—

She stills.

Nathaniel feels it instantly, the way she pulls back—not physically, but in some deeper, crueler way. He watches it happen in real time—the war inside her, the battle between love and self-preservation.

She swallows, her throat working as she tries to say something, but no words come.

And so, she does the only thing she can.

She pulls him closer again, her lips finding his, her hands threading into his hair with a frantic, almost reckless urgency.

Because if she speaks—

She will have to admit the truth.

And she is not ready to do that.

The club is warm, filled with the scent of brandy and cigar smoke, but Nathaniel feels none of it. His mind is elsewhere, stuck in the storm of last night—the taste of her, the way she had trembled in his arms, the way she had pulled away.

A chill runs through him, despite the heat of the fire crackling nearby.

"Nathaniel."

His valet's voice barely registers, until something—a folded slip of parchment—is pressed into his hand.

His brows knit together. "What is this?"

The man shrugs. "No signature. It was tucked inside your coat."

Nathaniel smooths out the paper, his heartbeat slowing—then stopping entirely.

She is in danger. Take her before it is too late.

His blood turns to ice.

His grip tightens around the note, his jaw locking as a sickening wave of certainty washes over him. He knew—he knew—Ashford was cruel. But this...

He doesn't think. He moves.

"Prepare the horses," he commands, his voice like steel. "We ride tonight."

He doesn't know who sent the warning. He doesn't care.

He only knows one thing:

He will not leave Evangeline in that monster's grasp.

Chapter Eight

The air in Ashford's estate is suffocating, thick with a tension Evangeline can no longer ignore. The grand chandeliers, the gilded mirrors, the lavish decor—it all feels like a gilded cage, trapping her in a place where she is nothing more than an ornament to be displayed, owned.

She feels his gaze before she sees him.

"Where were you last night?"

The words are smooth, polished, but they cut through the air like a blade. Ashford lounges in his chair, one hand idly swirling the amber liquid in his glass. His expression is unreadable, but his eyes—his eyes are razor-sharp, glinting with something that makes her stomach twist.

"Nowhere of importance," she lies, schooling her face into an expression of perfect indifference. She steps forward, intending to move past him, but before she can take another step, his fingers clamp around her wrist.

Cold. Unyielding.

Her breath catches as he yanks her back, his grip tightening—too tight, bruising.

"Do not lie to me, Evangeline," he murmurs, his voice deceptively soft. "I can smell the sin on your skin."

Her pulse skitters. He knows. Or, at the very least, he suspects.

She keeps her spine straight, meeting his gaze with as much defiance as she dares. "Release me."

Ashford's smile is slow, calculated. "You forget yourself, my dear." He pulls her closer, his breath hot against her ear. "You belong to me. And you will not humiliate me like some common whore."

The first blow comes fast. Too fast.

Pain explodes across her cheek, white-hot and blinding. She stumbles, her knees buckling, but before she can recover, another strike follows—harder, crueler. Her ribs scream in protest, a sharp, searing agony ripping through her.

She barely has time to react before he grips her by the hair, yanking her upright. Her scalp burns, her body protests, but she refuses to cry out.

"You will learn obedience," he hisses, his voice thick with venom. "One way or another."

Tears sting her eyes, but she won't let them fall. She won't give him that satisfaction.

But deep inside, a terrible realization settles.

This isn't the first time. And if she doesn't find a way out soon—it won't be the last.

The club is warm, filled with the scent of brandy and cigar smoke, but Nathaniel feels none of it. His mind is elsewhere, stuck in the storm of last night—the taste of her, the way she had trembled in his arms, the way she had pulled away.

A chill runs through him, despite the heat of the fire crackling nearby.

"Nathaniel."

His valet's voice barely registers, until something—a folded slip of parchment—is pressed into his hand.

His brows knit together. "What is this?"

The man shrugs. "No signature. It was tucked inside your coat."

Nathaniel smooths out the paper, his heartbeat slowing—then stopping entirely.

She is in danger. Take her before it is too late.

His blood turns to ice.

His grip tightens around the note, his jaw locking as a sickening wave of certainty washes over him. He knew—he knew—Ashford was cruel. But this...

He doesn't think. He moves.

"Prepare the horses," he commands, his voice like steel. "We ride tonight."

He doesn't know who sent the warning. He doesn't care.

He only knows one thing:

He will not leave Evangeline in that monster's grasp.

The air in the chamber is thick with tension, the dim candlelight casting long shadows against the walls. Evangeline barely has time to brace herself before Ashford's hand strikes across her face, sending her staggering back.

"You were speaking to him," he seethes, his voice low, trembling with fury. "What were you discussing?"

She straightens, her head held high despite the sharp sting on her cheek. "Nothing that concerns you."

His expression darkens, and before she can react, he grabs her wrist, yanking her toward the bed.

"What business do you have speaking to your former lover?" His grip tightens as he forces her down, pulling a length of silk from the bedpost and binding her hands. "Are you cheating on me, Evangeline?"

She glares at him, her breath shallow. "Let me go."

Ashford smirks, his fingers trailing down her trembling arms. "I hoped to make an obedient wife out of you." He leans in, his breath hot against her skin. "I took you back from the pits of hell, Evangeline. No one wanted you. You were discarded goods. And this is how you thank me?"

She clenches her jaw, refusing to give him the satisfaction of a reaction.

Ashford steps back, his movements slow, deliberate. "Fine," he mutters, unbuckling his belt. "Perhaps you need a lesson in gratitude."

The first lash lands with a crack, searing pain tearing through her back. She gasps but refuses to scream.

"Do you love him?" he demands.

Silence.

The second lash falls, sharper, crueler.

"ARE YOU FUCKING HIM?"

Evangeline bites down on her lip, her body trembling from the sheer force of the blow.

Ashford's grip tightens on the belt. His eyes gleam with fury. "Last time I'll ask nicely."

The third lash sends her forward, a sharp scream ripping from her throat as blood seeps from her torn skin.

He exhales slowly, adjusting the cuffs of his pristine white shirt, entirely indifferent to the agony he's just inflicted.

"There," he muses, smoothing down his waistcoat. "Perhaps now you'll understand your place."

He strides toward the door, his voice calm, almost bored. "No one enters this room until I return."

The maids, wide-eyed and trembling, nod frantically, their faces pale.

Ashford straightens his cuffs one last time and steps into the corridor, leaving Evangeline bound, shaking, and bleeding in the darkness.

Tonight, after all, was their engagement ball.

And he must show face.

Chapter Nine

Nathaniel stormed down the grand staircase of his estate, his pulse hammering like war drums in his ears. His fury had a life of its own, curling through his veins like fire, demanding blood. He barely acknowledged the footmen who scattered at the sight of his expression, nor did he register the sharp intake of breath from his steward as he barked out an order.

"Get my fastest horse ready. Now."

The guard stiffened, hesitating only for a breath. "My lord—" he began carefully, "the Duke of Ashford is hosting a ball tonight. A grand event in honour of his engagement."

Nathaniel's stomach turned to stone. A sickening, twisting knot of dread tightened in his chest.

A celebration? Tonight? After everything?

The urge to ride straight to Ashford's estate and end him with his bare hands nearly consumed him. But no. He needed to be careful. If Evangeline was still there, still in his clutches, he couldn't afford to lose control.

His jaw locked, breath ragged. "Saddle the horse. I ride to the ball."

Nathaniel rides harder than he ever has, pushing his horse through the storm-soaked roads.

She is there. Trapped. Hidden away.

And she is hurt.

The rain lashes against his skin, but all he feels is rage. If Ashford has sent men after her, if he so much as—

No. He will not think it.

He urges the horse faster. He will not be too late.

Nathaniel storms into the grand hall, his pulse hammering. The scent of expensive perfumes, champagne, and polished wood barely registers as his gaze sweeps over the glittering crowd.

He expects to see her—expects to see Ashford parading Evangeline around like a prized possession, gloating, displaying his victory.

But she isn't there.

His breath stills.

The room is alive with conversation, the soft hum of string instruments floating above the laughter and murmurs of the nobility. But Nathaniel sees only one man—Ashford.

The Duke stands at the center of the hall, lifting a crystal glass in a mockery of a toast, his mouth curled in that infuriatingly effortless smirk. A man at ease. A man revelling in his victory.

Nathaniel's hands clench into fists. Everything in him screams to end it here. To march across the ballroom, to wrap his hands around Ashford's throat, to watch the life drain from his eyes.

Not yet.

He swallows the rage, barely. He needs to be sure.

His movements are sharp, purposeful, as he turns on his heel. Where is she?

Then—

A young maid, lingering near the entrance, hands twisting

in her apron. She is watching the festivities with nervous, darting eyes.

Nathaniel strides to her. "Where is Lady Evangeline?"

The girl flinches, her gaze flicking to Ashford before she lowers her voice. "Her ladyship is unwell. She will not be in attendance."

The pieces fall into place.

Nathaniel breathes in sharply, his entire body going rigid. She is not here. Ashford did not announce it. He did not report her missing. Because he knows exactly where she is.

His hands curl into fists so tight that his nails bite into his palm.

Then—

"Lord Sinclair," a sultry voice purrs.

Nathaniel barely suppresses his irritation as Lady Beatrice Hargrove and Lady Eleanor Lytton step into his path, eyes gleaming with interest.

"You are looking particularly brooding tonight," Lady Eleanor observes coyly, trailing a gloved hand down the lapel of his coat.

"A man without a fiancée—so tragic," Beatrice adds, her lips curving. "It must be awfully lonely."

Nathaniel barely spares them a glance. Women have desired him for years. He has never cared less.

He steps past them without another word, his mind entirely consumed by one thought.

He has to get to her. Now.

Nathaniel rides like the wind, his cloak billowing behind him as he cuts through the storm-drenched night. The pounding of hooves against the muddy road echoes his own racing pulse. The storm is relentless, lashing against his face, but he does not slow. He cannot.

Ashford's estate looms ahead, a monstrous shadow against the stormy sky. A fortress of power, of cruelty, its towering stone walls slick with rain, the high iron gates cold and unyielding. Candlelight flickers through the tall windows, casting eerie glows against the storm-darkened walls. The estate is vast, opulent—but to Nathaniel, it is a prison.

The moment his horse skids to a halt in the courtyard, the tension is palpable. Ashford's servants are waiting. They know why he is here. A part of them is glad for it—but they dare not voice it.

A maid rushes toward him, her eyes wide with fear. "My lord, please—"

He brushes past her. He is done with words. His boots slam against the wet stone steps as he ascends, dripping with rain and fury.

"Where is she?" His voice is low, lethal.

The maid swallows, stepping back. "She—she needs rest, my lord. You cannot see her now."

Nathaniel does not slow. He moves through the halls with purpose, each step an unspoken warning. The air inside the estate is thick, stifling, as if the walls themselves hold their breath.

The butler steps forward, his expression carefully composed, hands raised in a futile attempt at control. "My lord, Lady Evangeline—"

Nathaniel seizes him by the collar and slams him against the wall. The butler gasps, his composure fracturing.

"Give. Me. The. Key."

"My lord—please—"

Nathaniel tightens his grip. "I will tear this house apart brick by brick if you do not hand me that key."

The butler's face drains of colour. His hands shake as he fumbles into his coat pocket, pulling out a single iron key. His fingers tremble as he places it in Nathaniel's palm.

Nathaniel does not wait.

He strides down the corridor, his breath ragged, his blood roaring in his ears. The moment he reaches the door, he shoves the key into the lock and forces it open.

The sight before him stops his heart.

Evangeline.

She is there.

Evangeline is sitting on the edge of the bed, her posture rigid, her hands clenched in her lap. She does not move. She does not react.

The clothes on her back are torn, the delicate fabric shredded and barely clinging to her frame. The dark stains of dried blood mar the fine silk. The belt—his belt—lies discarded in the corner, the leather stiff with what he already knows is her blood. A shattered mirror glitters on the floor beside it, the shards reflecting the dim candlelight in jagged, fractured pieces—much like her.

Nathaniel barely breathes.

She is shaking. Visibly. Violently.

His fists tighten, nails digging into his palm until pain slices through the haze of rage building inside him. He forces himself forward, step by step, his boots crunching against the broken glass.

Her body flinches at the sound.

God. What did he do to you?

Her face is a canvas of pain. A black eye blossoms along her cheekbone, dark and swollen, her lower lip split. Red streaks and bruises climb up her arms, her wrists raw and angry from restraints. The delicate skin at her ribs is marred with deep, ugly splotches of black and green.

Nathaniel clenches his jaw so hard it aches.

"Evangeline," he breathes, stepping forward. Gently. Carefully.

She flinches again. A small movement—but it wrecks him.

He stops in his tracks, his hands trembling at his sides. She is afraid of him.

The thought makes him sick.

"Did he do this to you?" His voice is raw, barely controlled.

She does not answer. She does not lift her gaze.

But she doesn't have to. Her silence is enough.

His throat tightens, his vision blurring at the edges.

He did this. Ashford did this. The man who dared to put his hands on her. The man who thought he could break her.

Nathaniel's rage is a living, breathing thing inside him. He wants blood. He wants to rip Ashford apart with his bare hands, to make him suffer, to make him bleed for every single mark he has left on her.

But all of that pales in comparison to the sight before him. She needs him.

He moves again, slower this time, lowering himself to one knee before her. "Evangeline," he whispers, his voice rough with restraint. "I was trying to save you."

She does not speak, does not meet his gaze again. But her breathing has changed—shallow, uneven. She is breaking, and it is killing him to watch.

A strangled breath escapes her, and then, in a whisper so fragile it nearly shatters him—"I wish you came sooner."

Her voice breaks, and so does she. A sob wracks her body, her shoulders shaking as she buries her face in his chest.

Nathaniel stiffens, stunned. His arms hover for the briefest second before he cups the back of her head, pulling her close, his fingers threading through her hair. He holds her—not as a lover, not as a man desperate for redemption—but as the only anchor she has left.

He presses his lips to the crown of her head, his jaw clenched so tight it aches. Rage burns in his chest, but he swallows it—for her. Now is not the time for vengeance. Now is the time for her.

"I'm here now," he breathes. "And I will never be too late again."

He exhales sharply, running a hand through his rain-drenched hair before lowering his voice, softer this time. "Please. Let me help you."

A muscle twitches in her jaw. Her fingers tighten against her lap. "You can't fix this, Nathaniel."

His breath hitches at the way she says his name, quiet, fractured, as though it costs her to speak it aloud.

"I can try," he murmurs. "If you let me."

She lets out a ragged breath, but she does not answer.

Finally, she lifts her gaze.

What he sees there—

It is not anger. It is not gratitude.

It is something far worse.

Nathaniel does not hesitate. He bends down, scooping Evangeline into his arms, her body limp against his chest. She barely reacts, her fingers weakly clutching at his coat as if grasping for something—anything—to hold on to. Her breath is shallow, her skin far too cold.

His heart slams against his ribs. She cannot stay here.

The moment he strides toward the door, the maids—huddled near the entrance—scatter in alarm. One, bolder than the rest, dares to step forward, her hands wringing nervously.

"M-My lord, please—"

"Get out of my way," Nathaniel snarls, his voice a razor's edge.

"But His Grace—"

He stops in his tracks, his rage boiling over. They dare speak of him now? After what he has done?

"IF I LEAVE HER IN THIS HOUSE OF WRETCHEDNESS, SHE WILL PERISH!" he roars, his voice reverberating through the vast halls. "PERHAPS NOT THIS NIGHT, BUT SOON ENOUGH—AND YOU BLOODY WELL KNOW IT!"

The maids flinch, exchanging frightened glances. None of them dare to argue.

Nathaniel storms past them, his grip on Evangeline tightening as he moves swiftly through the halls. The grand chandeliers, the marble floors, the towering portraits—all of it is insignificant. This place is nothing but a gilded prison.

The storm outside howls as he steps into the night, the rain drenching them both instantly. His horse waits, nostrils flaring, stamping against the muddy ground.

Carefully, he swings himself into the saddle, adjusting Evangeline in his arms before settling her in front of him. She stirs, just barely, her head lolling against his chest.

He grips the reins, his jaw set.

"Hold on," he murmurs, but she is too weak to respond.

With a sharp pull, he urges the horse forward. Away from this wretched place. Away from him.

And he does not look back.

Chapter Ten

Weeks pass, but time does nothing to mend the distance between them.

Nathaniel watches her, waiting, searching for something—anything—that might break through the walls she has built around herself. But Evangeline does not speak. She barely moves.

She is seated on the edge of the bed, her back impossibly straight, hands folded neatly in her lap. Poised. Detached. Distant.

Her face is unreadable, her gaze fixed on something beyond him, as if she is somewhere else entirely. A place he cannot reach.

"Evangeline," he tries again, his voice hoarse. "Say something. Anything."

Nothing.

The silence is unbearable. He would rather she scream at him, curse him, throw something, fight him—but she does none of those things.

His throat tightens as he runs a hand through his hair. He does not know how to fix this.

"Damn it, look at me!" The words rip from him, raw, desperate, an ugly sound in the heavy stillness between them.

She does not flinch, does not startle. She simply blinks—slow, indifferent.

This is worse than hatred. This is indifference.

Nathaniel kneels before her, his heart in his throat, his fingers curling into fists against the floor.

"I never meant for this," he breathes. "I never wanted to hurt you."

Finally, she speaks, but her voice is hollow, empty. "You say that as though it changes anything."

His gut twists. "I took you away from him—"

"And yet here I am," she cuts in sharply, finally looking at him, her gaze dull, lifeless. "Still a prisoner. Just with a different captor."

Nathaniel flinches as though struck.

He exhales sharply, standing, pacing like a caged animal. "I took you because I could not bear the thought of what he might do to you."

She laughs then—a brittle, joyless sound.

"What he might do?" She exhales a bitter laugh, shaking her head. "Nathaniel, you act as though taking me away now undoes everything. As though it erases the choices I made after you left me with none. I walked into his hands the moment society turned its back on me. The moment I had no future, no name, no protection."

She finally looks at him then, her gaze sharp with something colder than anger. "You were the first domino to fall. And I had no way of stopping the rest."

A sharp, piercing silence follows.

Nathaniel swallows hard, his hands flexing at his sides. He wants to say something—to argue, to promise her that she is safe now—but the words lodge in his throat. Because she is right.

He did this. Not Ashford. Him.

And he does not know how to make it right.

Nathaniel grips the edge of the chair beside him, his knuckles white, his entire body coiled with restrained emotion. He cannot bear this. Not her silence. Not her indifference. Not this haunting void between them.

"I will fix this," he vows, his voice low, raw. "I will make this right."

Evangeline finally moves. She lifts her chin, her expression impassive. "How?" she asks, her voice void of warmth. "By forcing me to stay here? By keeping me locked away until I finally forgive you?"

He steps closer. Too close.

"By giving you a choice," he murmurs. "For the first time since that night."

Her breath stills. Her mask falters.

He sees it then—the flicker of something beneath the cold exterior. Fear. Longing. Uncertainty.

"I love you," he says, raw, open, nothing hidden. "And I would rather burn than see you in his hands again. But if you tell me you want to go back to him, I will take you myself."

She looks at him for a long time. Searching.

Her fingers twitch against the fabric of her dress. She wants to believe him. She wants to believe in anything at all. But she has spent too long building walls—what happens if she lets them crumble now?

Finally, she speaks, and the words are a dagger to his chest.

"It does not matter what I want."

Nathaniel stares at her, his world cracking at the edges.

Because for the first time, he realises—*she wasn't waiting to be saved. She never believed she could be.*

He exhales sharply, his mind racing, his heart pounding as he takes a single step forward. "Evangeline," he says, his voice rough with urgency. "Think. The night you found me with Vivianne, you were supposed to be gone. You weren't meant to see any of it."

Her brows knit together in the smallest flicker of confusion, but she says nothing. She wants to dismiss it, to call it nonsense, but something gnaws at the back of her mind. A memory, hazy yet persistent. The way Ashford had found her that night—so soon, too soon. The way he had spoken of Nathaniel's betrayal, as if he had known before she had even told him.

Nathaniel kneels before her, hands braced against his thighs as he searches her face. "It all happened too perfectly, too conveniently. He paid Vivianne to be in my bed, and you—" He swallows, his throat tight. "You walked in at the worst possible moment. How do you think the news spread so quickly? Neither I nor Vivianne spoke a word of it. And yet, by morning, everyone knew."

Evangeline's fingers clench in her lap, her face paler than before. She looks down at her hands, at the way they tremble, as if they belong to someone else. It isn't possible. Is it? Her mind races, grasping at details she had ignored before. She wants to tell Nathaniel he's wrong, that he's reaching, but her throat is dry, the words refuse to come.

"And then what happens?" Nathaniel continues, his voice low and insistent. "Ashford is suddenly there, waiting in the wings like a saviour, sweeping you off your feet when you were at your weakest. He gave you a sense of protection, made you feel like you owed him something. And ever since, he has used that guilt to control you."

She tries to protest, but the words won't come.

Nathaniel watches her closely, his own chest rising and falling with the force of his emotions. He takes a half-step forward, then stops himself, his fingers twitching at his sides. He wants to touch her, to shake her, to make her see what he sees—but he cannot force this upon her. She must come to it herself. "This is not love, Evangeline," he says, his voice softer now, but no less certain. "This is control. He played you. He used your pain against you. He made you believe you were nothing without him."

For the first time since this conversation began, her lips part slightly, as if she might protest. But she doesn't. Because she cannot. The truth has settled in, unwelcome and undeniable. Her eyes widen—not with rage, not with hatred, but with something far more dangerous.

Realisation.

She stares at him, words dying on her tongue, her mind unraveling.

Why does he understand her so well? Why does he always see through her, even when she has tried so hard to disappear?

A war rages in her chest, the foundations of everything she thought she knew beginning to crack. And in that moment, for the first time in years—

She is afraid of the truth.

Chapter Eleven

The corridors were silent at this hour, the manor cast in shadow as Evangeline pressed herself against the cold stone wall, her breath barely audible. She had waited for this moment—for the household to slip into slumber, for Nathaniel's watchful gaze to wane. Now was her chance.

Barefoot, she moved swiftly, clutching the edges of her cloak tightly around her. The air outside was thick with the promise of rain, the scent of damp earth clinging to the night. The gates were ahead. Closer than before.

Her heart pounded. Every step carried her farther from the prison she had been placed in, but a shiver of unease crept down her spine. The world around her felt *too* still. The wind had stilled in the trees, the nocturnal calls of the forest absent. It was as if the night itself held its breath, watching her.

A single footstep crunched behind her.

Evangeline whirled, hands clenching. A hooded figure emerged from the shadows, the flickering lantern light barely illuminating their features. Before she could react, they reached forward and pressed something into her palm—a note, crisp and cool against her skin.

"*Do not trust what you see,*" the figure whispered before vanishing into the dark.

A warning.

She didn't have time to question it. Her pulse surged as she turned back toward the forest, but before she could move—

"Evangeline."

Nathaniel's voice cut through the night like a blade.

She stiffened.

She had been caught.

Nathaniel stood a few feet away, his dark coat billowing in the night breeze, eyes sharp with concern rather than anger. He did not approach her immediately, as if wary that she might bolt.

"Don't do this," he said, his voice softer than she expected. "Not like this."

Evangeline clutched the note in her trembling fingers, her breath uneven. She was prepared for rage, for accusations, but not this.

"I cannot stay here." Her words barely carried over the wind. "You cannot keep me here."

"I am not keeping you," Nathaniel countered, stepping closer. "I am protecting you."

She laughed bitterly. "Protection is just another cage."

His jaw tensed. "You do not understand—"

A distant sound broke the air. Hoofbeats. Many of them.

Evangeline's stomach twisted as the unmistakable sight of torchlight flickered through the trees. A group of riders emerged from the darkness, their presence commanding, their horses cutting through the mist like spectres of war.

Then came *him*.

Ashford sat astride a dark steed, his posture impeccable, his expression one of victorious amusement. "How kind of you to make this easy, Sinclair."

Nathaniel's body went rigid. He was far from the manor, and his guards were there also. His fingers flexed at his sides, his stance shifting into something prepared for battle. "You're outnumbered," Ashford continued smoothly. "Hand her over. She is not yours."

Evangeline flinched at his words. *Not yours.* As if she belonged to either of them. As if she had no say in her fate.

"I am engaged," she spat, forcing herself to look at Nathaniel. "You lost your chance when you chose another."

Nathaniel's eyes darkened. "Evangeline, I—You know that isn't true."

Her throat tightened, but before she could speak, she felt the air shift. The riders were closing in. Nathaniel was alone. Outnumbered. Fighting was not an option.

He knew it. She knew it.

His gaze met hers, something breaking behind his eyes. He didn't want to let her go. But he had no choice.

"This isn't over, Ashford!" Nathaniel roared as they seized her reins and turned her horse toward the path leading back to Ashford's estate.

Evangeline refused to look back.

But her heart remained behind.

The ride to Ashford's estate was long and silent, the weight of inevitability pressing down on Evangeline's shoulders. Rain had begun to fall, soft at first, then harder, pelting against her cloak as if the heavens themselves were weeping.

When they arrived at his London estate, the grand doors were already open, candlelight flickering from within. The moment her feet touched the marble floors, Ashford was waiting—smug, composed, every inch the man who believed he had won.

"You ran straight into my arms, my love." His voice was smooth, almost amused, as he stepped closer.

Evangeline's fingers curled into fists. "I am *not* yours."

Ashford tsked, shaking his head. "You wound me, dearest. You always have." He gestured vaguely to the room, the towering chandeliers casting sharp shadows against the walls. "Come now, you should be grateful. You are where you belong."

Her skin crawled. "I belong *nowhere* near you."

Ashford exhaled sharply, his mask of composure faltering just for a moment. "Evangeline, why do you resist me so?" His voice was quieter now, lacking the usual smugness, replaced with something resembling desperation. "I have given you everything—safety, a future, my devotion. Is that not enough? Can you not see that I have only ever wanted you to love me?"

He reached for her hand, but the instant his fingers brushed her wrist, she flinched away, a shudder running through her frame. The unspoken truth hung between them —his hands had not always been gentle.

Evangeline's eyes blazed with anger. "You *struck* me, Ashford. And you think I could ever love you after that?"

For the first time, something in his expression cracked. Defeat. Wounded pride. His fingers curled at his sides before he steeled himself once more. "You hesitate because of him," he accused, his voice laced with bitterness. "Sinclair has corrupted your mind against me. He's turned you against the only man who has ever truly cared for you."

He only smiled, as if she had said something charmingly naïve. Then, with a slow, deliberate movement, he plucked a folded letter from the table beside him. "Tell me, Evangeline, has Sinclair confessed yet?"

Her pulse quickened. "Confessed what?"

Ashford let out a quiet laugh, as if her ignorance amused him. "That the rumours about him were true, of course."

Evangeline clenched her jaw. "Rumours?"

"That he's a womaniser. That he preys upon women of good standing for sport." Ashford circled her like a predator. "Do you truly think you are *special* to him? That he is driven by some noble sentiment?" He leaned in, his breath warm against her ear. "Or are you simply another conquest?"

Evangeline's breath hitched.

She wanted to deny it. To tell Ashford that she knew Nathaniel, that she had *felt* his sincerity. But doubt twisted in her gut.

Ashford smiled, sensing her hesitation. "Think on it, my love. And when you realise the truth, you will see—there is only one man in this world who has ever truly wanted you."

She did not answer. But deep inside, her heart wavered.

Evangeline's breath came shallow and uneven as Ashford moved toward the ornate writing desk, the polished wood gleaming under the flickering candlelight. With a slow, deliberate motion, he picked up a folded letter, turning it between his fingers before holding it out to her.

"This," he murmured, "is something Nathaniel neglected to mention."

Evangeline hesitated before taking it, her pulse pounding as she unfolded the parchment. The inked words stared back at her, the handwriting strikingly familiar.

My Dearest Vivianne,

Every moment apart from you is unbearable. I ache for your presence, for the warmth of your embrace. You are the only one who truly knows me, who understands the restless hunger inside me. Evangeline—sweet, naive creature that she is—was never meant to hold my heart. She was a means to an end, a conquest to silence the doubters who thought I could never claim a duke's beloved as my own. But it is you I dream of, you I long for.

Soon, this charade will be over, and we will have all we deserve.

Wait for me until then.

Nathaniel Sinclair

Evangeline's hands trembled. "This... this is a lie."

Ashford chuckled, the sound infuriatingly calm. "Is it?" His voice dripped with feigned sympathy. "Did he never tell you? That he was the one who orchestrated your ruin for fun? Do you see why I want stand him? After everything he did to you, you still went back to him, do you not comprehend how that wounds me so?"

"No!" she snapped, shaking her head violently. "Nathaniel wouldn't—he couldn't—" Her breath hitched as she glared at the letter, as if by sheer force of will she could make the words vanish. "This is a forgery. It *must* be!"

Ashford sighed, stepping closer. "Oh, my dear, how much easier it would be if that were true. But the ink does not lie, nor does the hand that penned it. You know that is his writing, don't you?" He tilted his head, studying her reaction. "It was always a game to him, Evangeline. A challenge. What better way to cement his reputation than to prove he could take even a duke's betrothed?"

"You're lying!" Her voice cracked, her grip on the parchment so tight her knuckles whitened. "Nathaniel... he cared for me. I *felt* it."

"Ah, yes." Ashford smiled, mocking. "You *felt* it. But did he ever *say* it? Did he ever claim you as his own, in front of the world? Or did he keep you hidden, conveniently slipping away when it suited him?"

Evangeline's chest rose and fell in sharp bursts, her heart hammering. She wanted to hurl the letter at Ashford's smug face, to scream, to tear it apart—but the doubt had already taken root, curling around her like ivy in the dark.

"You can deny it all you wish, my love," Ashford murmured, watching her unravel, "but the truth always has a way of revealing itself."

She wanted to deny it. To tell Ashford that she knew Nathaniel, that she had *felt* his sincerity. But doubt twisted in her gut.

Ashford smiled, sensing her hesitation. "Think on it, my love. And when you realise the truth, you will see—there is only one man in this world who has ever truly wanted you."

Evangeline's fingers tightened around the fabric of her gown, her breathing uneven as she fixed Ashford with a sharp glare. "How did you find this letter?" she demanded, her voice edged with fury. "How do I know you didn't have it forged just to twist my thoughts?"

Ashford sighed, shaking his head, a flicker of something softer—something almost regretful—crossing his face. "When you became the talk of the ton a year ago, Evangeline, I was devastated. I had wanted your hand more than anything. I was smitten by your beauty, your grace... you were a woman of virtue, someone I wanted beside me." He exhaled slowly. "But by the time I sought to defend you, it was too late. The damage had been done. The whispers had spread like wildfire. Had I attempted to clear your name, it would have only looked like a desperate act—one staged by you or your father. Everyone would have thought, 'how convenient.'"

Evangeline swallowed hard, her anger warring with the ghost of something else. Pain. A deep, unfamiliar ache.

"So why tell me this now?" she pressed, her voice tight. "Why now, Ashford?"

His jaw tensed. "Because you deserve to know. And because I will not let Sinclair continue to weave his web around you."

She shook her head. "You hit me. Do you think I will forgive that?"

He stepped closer but did not touch her. "I regret it, Evangeline. My anger was not misplaced, but my actions were. I swear to you, it will never happen again." His voice was steady, filled with a conviction she did not want to believe. "I love you. I always have."

She swallowed, unable to look away as he continued. "I had one of my men pose as a customer at Vivianne's brothel," he admitted. "He searched her chambers and found this letter hidden in her dresser. I did not want to believe it myself, but once I read it, I knew. That was when I became determined to set things right."

Evangeline's grip on the letter wavered. Doubt warred with the truth she had clung to so fiercely. Had Nathaniel truly betrayed her?

And for the first time, she did not know.

The night was thick with tension, the air stifling with the weight of impending violence. The estate loomed in the distance, a beacon of his fury. Nathaniel's jaw clenched as he moved through the outer corridors, his boots crushing gravel with deadly purpose. The guards at the entrance barely had time to react before his blade sliced through the first man's throat. The second managed a choked warning before Nathaniel drove his dagger into his chest, twisting it until the resistance gave way.

Their bodies crumpled to the ground, staining the pristine marble steps with blood.

Nathaniel did not hesitate. He had come for one purpose, and he would let nothing stand in his way.

The grand doors to Ashford's estate burst open as he stormed inside, his soaked cloak dragging behind him like a shadow. The chandeliers flickered under the force of the storm outside, casting erratic beams of light across the vast hall. Servants scrambled out of his path, their whispers like ghosts in the corners of his mind.

He did not stop until he reached the doors to Ashford's study. With a forceful kick, they swung open.

And there she was.

Evangeline stood in the center of the room, the candlelight dancing across her delicate features. But she did not run to him. She did not cry out in relief. Instead, she took a step back, the distance between them suddenly an abyss.

Nathaniel's breath stilled. His rage had carried him here, but the sight of her hesitance froze him in place.

"Evangeline," he murmured, his voice thick with urgency. "I came for you."

She didn't answer immediately. Her fingers trembled as she clutched a letter to her chest. A single, damning piece of parchment.

His eyes flickered to it. Recognition struck him like a blade to the gut. He knew that letter—knew the handwriting all too well.

His own.

His expression darkened, his body coiling like a predator ready to strike. "Where did you get that?"

Evangeline's throat bobbed as she swallowed hard. "Ashford... he showed me." Her voice was barely a whisper, but it cut through him like thunder. "He said you orchestrated my ruin."

The weight of those words crushed Nathaniel's chest, but before he could speak, Evangeline's hand snapped up, trembling with fury. She lunged forward as if to slap Nathaniel, her emotions a whirlwind of rage and betrayal, but at the last second, she stopped herself. Her fingers curled into a fist as she took a deep breath, her body shaking with anger.

"I was *stupid* to trust you," she spat, turning her fury to Nathaniel. "Stories are not read backwards, and I know how ours ended the first time around. Why should this time be any different?"

Nathaniel's desperation was palpable. "Evangeline, please—"

"Enough!" she cut him off, stepping back toward Ashford. Nathaniel's entire body tensed as she pressed a hand against Ashford's chest, an unmistakable declaration. "Leave."

Ashford's smirk widened, but for the first time, his gaze held something more than amusement—confirmation. There *had* been something between them. This was not just possession or control. There was something deeper. And Nathaniel's presence had only cemented it.

Nathaniel's fists clenched, his breath uneven. "Evangeline—"

"I said leave," she repeated, steel in her voice. The room erupted into shouting—Nathaniel demanding she see reason, Ashford goading him further, and Evangeline standing firm between them. The storm outside howled as if mirroring the chaos within, but the one undeniable truth was clear: Ashford's hatred for Nathaniel deepened, and he had just won his most satisfying victory yet.

Nathaniel's fury burned white-hot. His fists clenched at his sides as his gaze darted to Ashford, who stood smugly by the fireplace, watching the scene unfold with sick satisfaction.

Evangeline's doubt was visible, raw and open on her face. He could see it—the war inside her, the desperate attempt to reconcile the man she had trusted with the monster she feared he might be.

"Tell me it's a lie." Her voice cracked. "Tell me you never wrote this."

Nathaniel took a slow, measured step forward. His heart hammered, not from battle, but from something far more dangerous—loss.

"I never wrote that," he said, voice low but unyielding. "And you know it."

Evangeline hesitated. Her grip on the letter loosened just slightly, but the poison of doubt had already seeped in.

Ashford's smirk widened, but beneath it, there was something else—something vulnerable, almost desperate. "It doesn't seem that way Sinclair," he challenged, but his voice faltered just slightly. "Prove to her that I am the villain in this tale. Prove to her that you are not the man that letter claims you to be."

He turned to Evangeline, his expression darkening with something closer to hurt than malice. "I wanted you to love me, Evangeline," he admitted, his voice quiet, but edged with frustration. "I wanted to give you the life you deserved. When the world tore you down, I tried to restore you, to make them see your worth again. But you—" he exhaled sharply, shaking his head. "You never gave me the chance. Because of him. Because of what he made you believe."

Nathaniel's eyes darkened, his muscles tensing. He would prove it.

And Ashford would pay for every second of this deception.

Chapter Twelve

The tension in the study was thick enough to suffocate. Candlelight flickered over the strained expressions of the two men standing on either side of Evangeline—one seething with barely contained fury, the other exuding an unsettling calm.

Nathaniel's fists clenched at his sides, his voice laced with venom. "You will regret ever touching her, Ashford."

Ashford merely smirked, pouring himself a glass of brandy from the decanter on the mantel. "Touch her?" he mused, swirling the amber liquid idly. "Nathaniel, you make it sound so sordid. I have merely given her what you could not—security, dignity, a future without scandal." He took a slow sip, watching Nathaniel over the rim of his glass. "It must wound your pride, knowing she turned to me in the end."

Nathaniel lunged forward, only stopping when Evangeline threw out an arm between them. "Enough!" she snapped, her voice slicing through the rising storm between them. Her breath was ragged, her chest heaving with emotion. "I will not stand here while you two fight like beasts over who owns me!"

Ashford lifted a brow but said nothing. Nathaniel swallowed hard, searching her face, but found no solace in her eyes. She was furious—at both of them.

She turned on Nathaniel first, her voice shaking with emotion. "You speak of regret, but do you have proof? Can you show me one thing that disproves this letter?" She thrust the damning parchment at him, her hands trembling. "Tell me, Nathaniel. Give me something—*anything*—that makes me believe you."

Nathaniel's jaw locked. He was trapped. He had nothing but his word, and after everything, it wasn't enough. His hands curled into fists as he exhaled sharply. "I swear to you, Evangeline, I never wrote that letter."

A bitter laugh escaped her lips, but it was laced with pain. "That's not proof."

She turned next to Ashford. "And you," she bit out, stepping toward him, "you claim to have done this for me? For my reputation? Then where is your proof? Where is your proof that you were the noble saviour you pretend to be?"

Ashford's smirk faltered for the briefest moment, but he recovered swiftly, setting down his glass with deliberate slowness. "My dear, proof is an amusing thing," he mused. "It is never so simple, is it?"

Evangeline's eyes flashed. "Then you have none either."

The room was electric, the air thick with unsaid words and burning accusations. Ashford's grip tightened behind his back as he studied her. Nathaniel, though burning with frustration, was quiet now, watching her, waiting for her next move.

Finally, Evangeline took a shuddering breath and straightened her shoulders. "You both think you can control me, that you can use my life as a battleground for your vendetta." She shook her head, voice hard with resolve. "I will not be a pawn in whatever war exists between you."

Ashford chuckled, low and indulgent. "You wound me, darling. I have only ever sought to protect you."

Nathaniel's eyes burned into Ashford, his voice deadly. "You don't protect things, Ashford. You *collect* them."

Evangeline turned away from both of them, wrapping her arms around herself as if holding herself together. Neither man had proof, and that alone was enough to make her stomach twist. Who was lying? Who was telling the truth? She had no answers.

For now, all she had was the sinking realization that the game had only just begun.

Nathaniel left heartbroken, the weight of betrayal crushing him with every step.

The house was silent, save for the faint ticking of the grandfather clock in the hallway. The night pressed heavily against the tall windows, the world outside drenched in shadows. Evangeline sat upright in bed, unable to sleep, her mind spinning with the accusations, the rage, the uncertainty.

Then, a rustling sound near the door.

She tensed, her breath catching. A small folded note had been slipped beneath the threshold. Heart hammering, she climbed out of bed, hesitated only a moment, then snatched it up. The wax seal was unfamiliar. She unfolded it with trembling fingers.

He isn't who you think he is. Look inside the book on his desk.

The words sent a shiver down her spine. Who had written this? Was it another of Ashford's tricks? Or a warning from someone else? A part of her hesitated. But another part— stronger, angrier—demanded answers.

Barefoot, she slipped through the darkened corridors of Ashford's estate, her pulse drumming in her ears. She knew these halls well by now, but tonight they felt different, ominous.

The study door loomed ahead. It was slightly ajar, the candle inside flickering weakly. Swallowing down her nerves, Evangeline stepped inside.

Her gaze swept across the room. The fireplace had long

since dimmed to embers, casting eerie, shifting shadows across the walls. And there, on the grand oak desk, sat a thick leather-bound book, just as the note had instructed.

She hesitated only for a second before stepping forward, fingers skimming over the worn cover. Her breath hitched as she pulled it open, flipping through pages until something unfamiliar slipped out—a folded letter, yellowed at the edges.

Her name was scrawled on the front.

But the handwriting—it was Ashford's.

Her stomach lurched as she unfolded it, her eyes darting over the words. The parchment trembled in her grip as she read:

To Whom It May Concern,

I, Evangeline Fairchild, must confess that my heart has never truly belonged to Nathaniel Sinclair. Though once bound by foolish sentiment, I have come to see the truth of his deceit. Nathaniel courted me not out of love, but out of conquest—a game played to satisfy his vanity and silence his critics. He spoke sweet lies, spun grand promises, but when it mattered most, he turned away.

It was not Nathaniel who saved me from disgrace, but the Duke of Ashford. I sought his protection, his wisdom, his strength. Where Nathaniel abandoned me to the whispers of society, Ashford extended his hand. I chose him of my own will, for in him, I see the future I was always meant to have. Let it be known that I harbor no ill will toward Nathaniel, only the regret of misplaced trust.

I write this to set the record straight. To free myself from the shackles of the past and embrace the security that only the Duke can provide.

- Evangeline Fairchild

A letter meant to bury Nathaniel once and for all.

The blood drained from her face. Ashford had been fabricating evidence against him. He had planned this, orchestrated every whispered lie, every piece of damning fiction. He had turned her entire life into a carefully crafted deception.

Her fingers curled into fists, crumpling the edge of the parchment. A deep, burning rage coiled within her chest.

The door creaked behind her.

She turned sharply, heart leaping into her throat.

Ashford stood in the doorway, his expression unreadable.

"You weren't supposed to see that," he murmured, stepping inside and closing the door behind him.

Evangeline's grip tightened around the letter. "You lied to me."

His lips pressed into a thin line, his composure faltering for the first time. "I did what was necessary," he insisted, his voice rough with emotion. "You don't understand—I had no other choice. I *had* to protect you."

Evangeline's fury flared hotter. "Protect me?" she hissed. "By forging a letter in my name? By turning me against Nathaniel? You manipulated me, twisted everything—and for what? To win?"

Ashford's expression darkened, but his voice softened, almost pleading. "Because I love you, Evangeline. I always have. I watched them tear your name apart a year ago, and I couldn't bear it. I tried to fix it, but by the time I moved, it was too late. If I had spoken then, they would have dismissed me as a desperate suitor trying to rewrite history. No one would have believed me. No one would have believed *you*."

She swallowed hard, the anger warring with something dangerously close to uncertainty.

"I only wrote that as a last resort," he continued, stepping closer, desperation creeping into his tone. "Everything else I've told you was true. Nathaniel doesn't deserve you. He will ruin you, just as he did before. I *could not* stand by and watch it happen again."

She let out a sharp, bitter laugh. "And I'm supposed to believe that? After everything? After you hit me?"

His features twisted in something like regret. "I lost control. But my anger was not misplaced. You were about to throw yourself back into his arms and undo everything. I won't apologise for wanting to save you."

Evangeline stared at him, her pulse pounding. "You don't want to save me, Ashford. You want to own me."

Ashford's jaw clenched. He took another step forward, but this time, she didn't back away. Her fingers tightened around the letter, and she met his gaze with unshaken defiance.

The game had changed. And now, she wasn't playing by his rules anymore.

Ashford's gaze softened as he stepped toward her, the firelight casting shadows across his face. His usual smirk was absent, replaced by something raw, something vulnerable.

"Evangeline," he murmured, his voice a plea. "I know I've made mistakes, but everything I've done—every lie, every desperate act—it was all for you. I cannot bear to lose you."

She remained still, frozen between the weight of his words and the cold certainty in her chest.

He reached for her, cupping her face in his hands. "Say you see it now. Say you know I only wanted to protect you. I love you, Evangeline. More than my own life."

She wanted to recoil, but she couldn't. Not with the fire of his gaze locked onto hers, not with the knowledge that if she pushed him too far, she might unleash something even darker within him.

When he kissed her, she did not pull away.

His lips moved against hers, slow and tender at first, but there was desperation beneath the surface. A need to claim, to own. She allowed it. She let him kiss her, let him thread his fingers through her hair and press her against him. But inside, she was empty. Hollow.

When he carried her to the bed, she did not resist. When he undid the ties of her gown, she did not stop him. She stared at the ceiling as he whispered sweet words against her skin, words she no longer believed. She closed her eyes, waiting for it to be over, waiting for morning.

He thought he had won.

But deep inside, Evangeline knew—this was not surrender. This was survival.

The night air was sharp against Evangeline's skin as she raced through the stables, her breath coming in short, frantic gasps. Ashford lay deep in sleep, his features slack and peaceful in a way that made her stomach turn. Pity and revulsion tangled within her as she turned away from him, her heart hammering with conviction.

She could not stay.

In nothing but her undergarments, she saddled a horse, ignoring the bite of cold against her exposed skin. She had wasted too much time already. Digging her heels into the beast's sides, she bolted into the night, her only thought on one thing—Nathaniel.

The darkness stretched before her, vast and unforgiving, but she did not slow. The wind whipped through her hair, her pulse pounding in tandem with the thundering hooves beneath her. She prayed she wasn't too late.

Then, in the distance, she saw him.

"Nathaniel!" she screamed, her voice breaking against the night.

His horse jerked to a stop. For a moment, he did not turn. Evangeline felt her heart seize as she urged her horse forward. "Please, wait!"

Slowly, he turned in the saddle, his face shrouded in shadow.

"Go back, Evangeline." His voice was hoarse, exhausted. "There's nothing left to say."

"That's not true!" she cried. "I was wrong—I didn't believe you, and I should have. I was a fool to doubt you."

Nathaniel exhaled sharply, shaking his head. "You weren't

a fool. You were right to question me. And now, you have your future. With *him*." He spat the last word with quiet venom, his grip tightening around the reins. "I won't stand in your way. I want you to be happy. And I'm sorry that I've only been a stain on your engagement."

Her frustration boiled over. "You *always* do this," she snapped. "You let me go so easily. You never fought for me. Not the way I needed you to."

Nathaniel's jaw clenched. "I *tried,* Evangeline! But you didn't reciprocate. Do you know what it was like? Watching you slip away while I stood there with my hands tied? You made your choice."

"And you made it simple by never giving me a reason to stay!" she shot back, the rawness in her voice cutting through the night. "You cheated, Nathaniel. You left me alone in the worst moment of my life. And when the scandal broke, where were you? You let me suffer!"

The silence between them was deafening, charged with years of unspoken wounds. His eyes burned into hers, fury and anguish warring within them.

Finally, he spoke, his voice like gravel. "You think I didn't want to fight for you? That I didn't *love* you enough to stand by you? I did. But you never *let* me. And that—" he let out a bitter laugh, "—that is what hurts the most."

Tears blurred her vision. "Then why are you letting me go now? Why are you *still* letting me go?"

His fingers flexed around the reins as if physically restraining himself from reaching for her. "Because you doubted me. Even now, I see it in your eyes. You don't *trust* me."

She flinched, his words slicing through her like a blade.

Their horses carried them to his manor, the argument still raging between them. The tension thickened as they reached the door, their anger raw and unfiltered.

"Say it," Nathaniel growled, stepping closer. "Say you trust me. Say you *believe* in me."

Evangeline's breath hitched. She *wanted* to. But after everything...

She couldn't.

Nathaniel exhaled sharply, his body taut with restraint. He needed to hear it, to *know* the truth buried beneath her hesitation. He stepped forward, pressing her, voice thick with frustration. "Say it, Evangeline. Say that you still love me."

Her heart pounded, her breath uneven. She *wanted* to, but the fear twisted inside her, holding her tongue captive. "I can't —" she whispered, shaking her head. "Swear to me that you would never hurt me again. That you will fight for me now and forevermore."

Nathaniel's gaze flickered with something unreadable before it softened, filled with a realization that struck him to his core. He put himself in her place, saw the pain she had endured, the fight she had wanted him to give long ago. He had let her go too easily before. He would not make the same mistake again.

His voice, rough with emotion, steadied. "I swear it. I will be loyal to you until the end of my days. No force, no person, nothing in this world will ever make me let you go again."

Evangeline gasped, her hand flying to her mouth, overwhelmed. Her heart raced, her resolve breaking under the weight of his words. He saw it, saw the vulnerability in her eyes, the way she trembled not from fear—but from something far deeper.

Nathaniel took a step closer, his voice lower now, prophetic in its conviction. "You rode through the night to find me. You faced the cold, the storm, because you knew this isn't over. Because no matter what, you have always been mine. And I, yours."

Evangeline shuddered, the truth of it sinking into her

bones. "I never stopped loving you," she whispered, barely more than a breath.

Thunder rumbled in the distance, and as the rain fell, they stood there, unmoving. Nathaniel studied her, taking in her damp hair, her flushed cheeks, the rawness in her gaze. She looked so exposed, so undone—and in that moment, something inside him shattered.

With a sharp inhale, he lunged.

His mouth claimed hers with a fierce, desperate intensity, defiant and unyielding. It wasn't just a kiss—it was desperation, a reclamation, an unrelenting need to prove that this time, he would not let go. His hands tangled in her hair, pressing her closer, deepening the kiss as the rain poured over them.

Evangeline melted into him, grasping his collar, her breath hitching as his body pressed against hers. She had waited so long for this—too long. And now, as the storm raged around them, she finally let herself believe in what had always been theirs.

As the kiss broke, Nathaniel rested his forehead against hers, his breath heavy. "Then let's stop pretending we can walk away from this," he murmured, brushing damp strands of hair from her face.

Evangeline nodded, breathless. The night was far from over. And neither was their story.

Nathaniel carried her from the entrance, the rainwater drenching both their clothes, clinging to them like the remnants of a past neither could escape. His arms were firm around her, steady despite the storm raging outside. As he lifted her effortlessly, his eyes shone with something that made her breath catch—pure, undiluted love.

Evangeline let out a surprised laugh, breathless from the suddenness of it all. The warmth of his body seeped through the wet fabric, grounding her in a way she hadn't expected.

"Nathaniel," she murmured, her fingers tightening slightly in his shirt.

He smiled down at her, the corners of his lips curling with devotion. "I have you," he whispered, carrying her inside the manor, away from the storm.

The candlelight flickered in the bedroom, casting golden hues against the damp skin of her arms as he laid her gently on the bed. His gaze roamed her face, lingering on the flush of her cheeks, the way her undergarments clung to her, exposing the peaks of her breasts. But it wasn't lust that burned in his eyes —it was reverence.

His fingers traced the edge of her gown, moving to undress her, but she stiffened, a shadow of hesitation crossing her face.

Nathaniel stilled, his expression softening as he realised. "Eva...?"

She lowered her gaze, her hands instinctively covering the faint bruises on her arms, remnants of Ashford's cruelty. Shame burned through her, and she whispered, "I... I don't know if you should see me like this."

Nathaniel cupped her face, tilting it gently so that their eyes met. "Nothing about you could ever change the way I desire you," he murmured, brushing his thumb over her cheek. "I want to show you what it means to be loved. To be cherished. To be *safe*."

Evangeline swallowed hard, her heart thundering. "You're not going anywhere?"

His gaze turned fierce. "Never."

She released a shaky breath, and her hands fell away, allowing him to slowly slide her garment off her shoulder. His lips found the curve of her neck, pressing soft, reverent kisses down to the bruised skin. When she flinched slightly, he pulled back, whispering, "Tell me if it's too much."

She shook her head, overwhelmed by his tenderness. "No... I just..." She hesitated, but before she could finish, Nathaniel pressed his lips to each bruise, kissing them as though his love alone could erase the pain.

She gasped at the gentleness of it. Tears welled in her eyes as realization struck—Nathaniel had never been the villain. He had always been the man who would fight for her, who would love her despite the damage, despite the scars.

He reached up, his hand sliding to the nape of her neck, tilting her face toward his. Their lips met, soft and slow this time, a promise sealed between them. She sat upright in the bed, facing him fully, and her hands hesitantly touched his chest, feeling the warmth of his body through the damp fabric.

Nathaniel was still clothed, and her shyness overtook her. As he gently lowered the soaked undergarment, revealing more bruises along her ribs, she instinctively covered herself, looking away. "Do I look awful to you? It's okay if you think so."

Nathaniel's fingers brushed over her knuckles, easing them away from her body. His eyes darkened—not with pity, but with something deeper, something unbreakable. "Evangeline," he whispered, "you are breathtaking. Every inch of you."

A soft whimper escaped her lips as he flicked her nipple, teasing, worshiping her with his mouth, trailing kisses over her heated skin. She arched under his touch, her worries slowly melting away under the weight of his love. His lips traveled lower, teasing, tasting, until she was lost in him completely.

Nathaniel pulled back only for a moment, his breath warm against her thigh. "Tonight is for you," he whispered, voice hushed yet fervent. "I only want you to feel pleasure. Let me take away everything else."

Evangeline let her head fall back, surrendering to the warmth of his devotion. She had never known tenderness like this.

And as Nathaniel worshiped her, she knew, without a doubt, that she had found home in him once more.

Evangeline woke to the soft glow of morning light filtering

through the heavy curtains. For a fleeting moment, she had forgotten where she was—forgotten the events of the night before. But as she stretched beneath the luxurious sheets, the ache in her body and the warmth lingering on her skin told her it had been real.

Nathaniel was gone.

Her heart twisted in panic for a moment, but before she could even sit up, the door creaked open. There he stood, holding a silver tray, the scent of fresh bread, warm honey, and tea filling the air.

She blinked. *A Viscount... bringing me breakfast?*

Nathaniel caught her expression and smirked as he strode forward, setting the tray down beside her. "You look as if you've seen a ghost."

She shook her head in disbelief, staring at the tray. "You —*you*—carried this from the kitchen yourself? Do you have any idea what the maids must be thinking?"

He gave a careless shrug, settling onto the edge of the bed. "Let them think what they will. I am proud of what we share, Evangeline."

Her lips parted, surprised by his ease. "But you—your reputation—"

"What use is a reputation if I cannot do this for the woman I love?" he cut in smoothly, eyes gleaming with certainty.

She swallowed hard, reaching hesitantly for a slice of bread. "I don't know what to say."

"Say you'll eat before it gets cold," he teased, nudging the tray closer.

A smile tugged at her lips, but it faltered. She lowered the bread and looked at him, regret flickering in her gaze. "I never should have doubted you. I should have believed you."

Nathaniel exhaled, shaking his head. "It's done, Evangeline. What matters is that you're safe now."

Safe. But not entirely. She hesitated before voicing the

truth neither of them could ignore. "I'm still engaged to Ashford."

The lightheartedness in his expression dimmed. A shadow crossed his face, but he remained calm. "Not for long."

She furrowed her brows. "Nathaniel..."

He hesitated for only a moment before finally revealing, "I have an informant inside Ashford's circle."

Her breath caught. "Who?"

He shook his head. "I don't know. They only leave notes. Anonymous warnings."

Evangeline's fingers tightened around the edge of the tray. "Nathaniel... I—I think there's something else you should know. Strange things have been happening to me."

His eyes sharpened. "What do you mean?"

She hesitated, uncertainty pooling in her stomach. "The night when I ran away from your manor," she said softly, "someone cloaked came behind me to warn me not to believe everything I see."

Nathaniel's expression darkened. "And you're only telling me this now?"

"I didn't know what to make of it. And then later... the same figure slipped a note into my dresser. It told me to investigate a letter in Ashford's study. That's how I found out about the forgery."

Nathaniel's jaw tightened. "So someone is playing their own game inside Ashford's walls. But why?"

Someone inside Ashford's world was working against him—but for what purpose?

Evangeline remained in bed, her fingers lightly tracing the rim of the teacup Nathaniel had brought her. The warmth of the morning had turned cold with the weight of their conversation, and though the room was still filled with the scent of fresh bread and honey, all she could taste was the bitter truth between them.

Nathaniel stood at the window, his expression taut, his shoulders tense. "We have to leave London, Evangeline."

She frowned, setting the cup aside. "Leave?"

He turned to face her, his jaw set with quiet determination. "Ashford will not let this go. His pride is too great. You humiliated him, and he will want to restore his so-called *honor*. And I fear that means he'll stop at nothing." His voice lowered, thick with restrained fury. "If I must fight him, then so be it. But I won't have you in harm's way."

Evangeline sat up straighter, her brows drawing together. "You don't get to decide my life, Nathaniel."

His eyes burned into hers. "Then decide now. Because staying means dying."

A silence stretched between them, heavy and charged. She should have been afraid. But she wasn't. Not of Ashford. Not of the danger that loomed over them. What she feared—what she *knew*—was that she couldn't be apart from Nathaniel again. Not after everything.

"I won't leave you," she said, her voice unwavering. "If Ashford wants a fight, then we face him together."

Nathaniel exhaled sharply, as if grappling with both frustration and admiration. "Evangeline—"

"No." She swung her legs over the bed and stood, walking toward him with quiet resolve. "I have spent too long letting others decide my fate. I won't be a prisoner to fear, not anymore."

His hands reached for her arms, holding her gently. "I just want to keep you safe."

"Then don't send me away. Fight for me *with* me."

Nathaniel searched her face, his grip tightening before he suddenly stepped back. He turned to the window, his hands braced against the frame, his head hanging forward. He let out a slow, controlled breath, but Evangeline saw the tension in his shoulders—the war raging inside him.

"Evangeline, I don't know if I can do this," he admitted,

his voice rough. "I've failed you before. I thought protecting you meant keeping you away from danger, but I see now—I see you standing here, ready to fight, and I realise I've been wrong this whole time."

She remained silent, letting him find his words, watching as he forced himself to face her once more.

"Protecting you doesn't mean shielding you from everything. It means standing beside you. Fighting *with* you," he said, his voice stronger now, filled with certainty. "I won't make the same mistake again." His grip tightened just slightly, his forehead pressing against hers. "Together then. Until the end."

Evangeline closed her eyes, relief and determination washing over her. The storm was coming, but she would face it with him. They would not run.

They would fight.

Chapter Thirteen

The wind howled through the barren trees, the sky above them blackened with the promise of an unrelenting storm. Nathaniel gripped the reins tightly, guiding their horses through the thickening rain. Evangeline held on behind him, her cloak soaked through, her fingers frozen as they clutched at his waist.

They had ridden for hours, pushing through the relentless cold, knowing they had no choice but to leave London behind. Now, as the storm raged in full force, Nathaniel spotted a structure through the curtain of rain—a hunting lodge, long abandoned, nestled between the trees.

"We'll stop here," he called over the wind, guiding the horses toward shelter.

The moment they dismounted, Evangeline's legs wobbled from exhaustion. Nathaniel caught her by the waist, steadying her. "Inside. Now."

She wanted to argue, to insist she wasn't that weak, but the biting wind stole the words from her lips. Without another word, she rushed through the door, shivering violently as Nathaniel followed behind, slamming it shut against the roaring storm.

The lodge was cold, the air inside stale from disuse. Nathaniel immediately set to work, tossing aside old furniture, searching for anything that could be used to start a fire. Evangeline stood near the door, drenched and breathless, watching as he worked with ruthless efficiency.

Finally, the fire caught, crackling to life in the stone hearth. A flickering glow spread across the space, but it did little to warm the tension between them.

They were alone.

Trapped.

Soaking wet.

Freezing.

Evangeline wrapped her arms around herself, staring at the flames, pretending she didn't notice the way Nathaniel's eyes kept flicking toward her, or how her heart pounded at the thought of them stranded together in this tiny, intimate space.

Nathaniel stood, peeling off his drenched coat with a sigh. "We'll need to get out of these wet clothes before we freeze," he muttered, tossing it aside.

Evangeline swallowed hard as he pulled his shirt over his head, the firelight casting golden hues over his bare skin. Water still clung to him, trailing down the hard planes of his chest, disappearing beneath the waistband of his trousers.

She tore her gaze away, refusing to acknowledge the heat rising up her neck.

Nathaniel smirked. "You can keep looking, Evangeline. I don't mind."

She turned sharply, glaring at him. "I wasn't looking."

His smirk deepened. "Liar."

She huffed, crossing her arms, but the movement only made her more aware of how her own clothes clung to her skin, her damp chemise nearly sheer in the firelight.

Nathaniel's gaze flicked lower, darkening. "You should undress, too. You're shivering."

Evangeline stiffened. "I'm fine."

Nathaniel stepped closer, his voice dropping to something smoother, more dangerous. "Are you?"

Tension crackled between them, sharp as the storm outside. She knew this game, knew the way he could unravel her with just a look. But she was stronger now. She wouldn't fall so easily.

So she lifted her chin, meeting his gaze with quiet defiance. "Yes."

Nathaniel exhaled a short laugh, shaking his head as he turned back to the fire. "Very well, my lady. But don't think I don't see it."

"See what?"

He looked over his shoulder, his smirk lazy, confident. "The way you want me."

Her breath caught, her fingers clenching into her skirts. "You are insufferable."

"And you are still staring."

Evangeline forced herself to look away, but the damage was done. The storm outside wasn't the only one they had to weather tonight.

The tension between them stretched, thin as glass, ready to shatter. The fire crackled, casting golden light over Nathaniel's bare chest, over Evangeline's damp skin, her chemise clinging to every curve.

He moved first.

A step. Then another. And then she was in his arms.

His mouth found hers in a fierce, unrelenting kiss, a collision of heat and unspoken longing that had been waiting to break free. It was not just hunger but desperation, a need that had been buried beneath years of pain and stubborn resistance. Evangeline gasped against him, her fingers threading through his damp hair, gripping as if he were the only thing tethering her to the present.

Nathaniel's hands mapped her body as he guided her down onto the rug, his touch reverent yet insistent. The fire cast flickering golden hues over them, illuminating every shiver, every sharp inhale as he explored her with slow, deliberate care. His lips traced down her throat, across her collarbone, marking a path as though memorizing her—every curve, every tremble beneath his fingertips. He whispered against her skin, words she couldn't quite make out, words she wasn't sure she needed to hear.

This was different.

There was no battle here, no resistance—only surrender. No hesitancy, no past regrets weighing them down. Only the present, only this moment, only *them*.

It was different this time.

No urgency. No doubt. Just them, surrendering to what had always been inevitable.

Her name was a reverent whisper on his lips as he made love to her, his touch slow, consuming, a promise etched into every movement. She clung to him, tears pricking at the corners of her eyes, overwhelmed by the depth of it all.

And when it was over, she turned away.

Nathaniel reached for her, but she curled into herself, her back to him, her walls still standing.

He exhaled a quiet breath, pressing a kiss to her shoulder before pulling her against him, even as she resisted.

Even as she remained silent.

The storm outside had begun to fade, but inside her, another had only just begun.

The fire had burned low, casting only a faint glow across the cabin walls. Dawn was breaking, a dim, grey light seeping in through the cracks in the wooden shutters. Nathaniel lay awake, his body still warm from the night before, but his mind restless.

Evangeline slept beside him, her back to his chest, the rise and fall of her breathing slow and even. He watched her in the quiet, memorizing the delicate curve of her shoulder, the way a strand of her hair had fallen across her cheek. This woman

—*his* woman—had undone him in ways he never thought possible.

But what did this mean?

For a moment, he allowed himself the fantasy—that they could stay here, hidden away from the world, from duty, from Ashford. But reality was unrelenting. Their stolen moment of peace would not last.

With a sigh, Nathaniel sat up, running a hand through his tousled hair. He reached for his trousers, pulling them on as he moved toward the door. The storm had passed, leaving behind a world damp with fresh rain. The air was crisp, and for a moment, all seemed still.

Until he saw it.

A folded piece of parchment, lying in the center of the wooden floor—*inside* the locked cabin.

Nathaniel's blood ran cold. Slowly, he bent to pick it up, his fingers tightening around the rough paper as he turned it over. The handwriting was the same as before, scrawled and urgent.

He knows where you are.

His pulse roared in his ears.

Nathaniel turned sharply, his eyes darting to Evangeline still curled beneath the blankets, unaware of the silent threat that had found them even here.

They were not safe.

And now, there was no doubt.

Ashford was coming.

Nathaniel's eyes drifted from the note in his hands, his mind racing through the implications. Then—

A sound. Subtle, but there. A shift in the air, the faintest creak of a floorboard.

Footsteps.

His instincts screamed at him, but before he could move, a shadow loomed over him. Cold steel pressed against his throat.

Nathaniel reacted on instinct, jerking to the side just as the dagger sliced across his skin. He rolled away, crashing into the wooden table, sending a chair tumbling. His breath was ragged as he took in the figure before him—a man, cloaked in darkness, his face obscured, blade glinting in the dim light of dawn.

Nathaniel's weapon lay across the room, near the fireplace. Too far.

He had no choice but to fight barehanded.

Evangeline's scream shattered the silence. "Nathaniel!"

The intruder lunged again. Nathaniel dodged, barely, pain searing his ribs as the blade sliced against his side. He grappled with the assassin, fists landing blows, but the man was trained, precise, ruthless. Nathaniel was losing ground.

Pinned, breath coming in ragged gasps, he saw the dagger poised above him—ready to end it all.

Then—

Evangeline.

She stood frozen for half a second, eyes wide with terror before something shifted—something primal, desperate. Her gaze darted to the fireplace. Nathaniel's sword.

Without thinking, she lunged, fingers wrapping around the hilt. It was heavy, but she didn't care. She ran toward Nathaniel, heart pounding, desperately fighting for his life. Just as the assassin drove the dagger downward, she lunged forward and plunged Nathaniel's sword into the man's back.

The steel pierced through flesh, through bone.

The assassin stiffened. A strangled noise escaped him, his body jerking as Evangeline yanked the sword free. Blood sprayed onto the wooden floor as he crumpled, lifeless.

Silence fell.

Evangeline stood there, trembling, the sword slipping from her fingers. Her breath was ragged, her chest heaving as she spat onto the ground, fury and shock warring in her expression.

"I have endured too much to lose you now."

Nathaniel, still frozen on the floor, stared at her, his

expression unreadable. Then, slowly, he rose, stepping toward her.

"Evangeline..."

Her hands shook. "I— I killed him."

Nathaniel reached out, cupping her face in his hands, his thumb brushing against her cheek. "You saved my life."

Tears welled in her eyes, but she refused to let them fall. "I didn't even think. I just—"

"You *acted*." His voice was steady, grounding. "You were brave."

She swallowed hard, nodding, but her body still trembled. Nathaniel exhaled, pressing a kiss to her forehead, lingering there, as if silently thanking her.

He pulled back, eyes burning with emotion. "We need to go. Now."

Evangeline took a shaky breath, steeling herself. "Then let's go."

She wasn't running anymore.

Not from this. Not from him. Not from the fight ahead.

The rush of adrenaline had barely faded when Evangeline noticed the crimson seeping through Nathaniel's shirt. Her breath caught as she stepped forward, fingers trembling as she touched the torn fabric. The wound wasn't fatal, but it was deep—bleeding heavily, staining his skin and the floor beneath him.

"We need to stop the bleeding," she said urgently, glancing around the cabin for anything that might help.

"We need to keep moving," Nathaniel countered, his voice strained.

Evangeline shot him a glare. "You're not going anywhere until I tend to this."

He opened his mouth to argue but sighed, relenting as he lowered himself onto a chair near the fireplace. Evangeline ripped a piece of cloth from her underdress, moving with quick, purposeful hands as she pressed it against his side.

Nathaniel hissed through his teeth. "You always were stubborn."

"And you always were reckless," she shot back, focusing on binding the wound.

For a moment, there was only silence between them, save for the crackling of the fire and the storm still howling outside. Then, softer, Nathaniel spoke.

"I'm proud of you."

Evangeline stilled for a fraction of a second before resuming her work. "Proud of me for what?"

"For what you did. For not hesitating." His voice was filled with something deep, something raw. "You saved my life."

She exhaled sharply, shaking her head. "It was him or you, Nathaniel. There was no choice."

"There's always a choice," he said, watching her. "And you chose me."

She refused to meet his gaze, her hands tightening the bandage. "Of course, I did."

Nathaniel reached for her wrist, stilling her movements. "Look at me."

Reluctantly, she did. His expression was unreadable, but his eyes burned with emotion.

"I know what it took for you to do that," he murmured. "And I know what it will cost you to live with it."

Evangeline swallowed, her throat tight. "I don't regret it."

His lips curved, not quite a smile, but something close. "I know."

She sighed, sitting back on her heels. "I hate him."

Nathaniel raised a brow. "Who?"

"Ashford." The name tasted bitter in her mouth. "He did this. He sent that man to kill you."

Nathaniel's expression darkened. "He was always a coward. Always one to let others do his dirty work."

Evangeline let out a harsh laugh, shaking her head. "I

knew he was cruel, but this? Hiring a man to slit your throat in your sleep?"

Nathaniel exhaled, tilting his head back against the chair. "This is about more than honor for him now. It's about control. And you... you were never meant to escape him."

Evangeline's jaw tightened. "I am not his. I never was."

Nathaniel's fingers brushed against her cheek, his touch light, reverent. "I know."

The storm raged outside, but inside, wrapped in the glow of the fire, there was only them. Wounded but alive. Bruised but unbroken.

And more determined than ever to end this once and for all.

The wind howled against the cabin walls, rattling the shutters as Evangeline tightened the last knot on Nathaniel's bandage. His skin was warm beneath her fingertips, his breath slightly ragged from pain, but he remained still, watching her as she worked.

Then—

A knock.

Sharp. Precise.

Both of them froze.

Nathaniel's hand moved instinctively toward the nearest weapon, his jaw clenched. Evangeline's pulse hammered in her throat as she exchanged a glance with him, unspoken tension stretching between them.

No one should have been able to find them here.

Nathaniel stood slowly, careful of his injury, his muscles tensed like a predator waiting to strike. Evangeline rose beside him, her breath caught in her chest as another knock echoed through the cabin—this time softer, more deliberate.

Whoever it was... they weren't leaving.

Nathaniel's grip tightened around the hilt of his dagger as he stepped forward, pulling the door open just enough to see beyond the threshold.

A figure cloaked in shadows stood before them, rain dripping from the hem of their hood. Then, slowly, they lifted their head, revealing a familiar face beneath the dim light of dawn.

Vivianne.

Evangeline's breath left her in a rush.

Nathaniel stiffened beside her, his fingers curling into a fist.

She shouldn't be here.

Vivianne's gaze flickered between them before she exhaled, voice calm, measured.

"We need to talk."

Vivianne stepped inside, breathless, her cloak clinging to her from the rain. Her chest rose and fell rapidly, evidence of how long she had been running. Evangeline watched her cautiously, arms crossed, while Nathaniel remained tense, jaw locked tight.

"How did you know where we were?" Nathaniel demanded, his tone sharp.

Vivianne hesitated, shifting her weight, her fingers twisting in her cloak. "Because I was looking for you all night. I *had* to find you."

Nathaniel's eyes narrowed. "That's not an answer."

Vivianne's mouth pressed into a thin line. "Nathaniel, please. I came to warn you. You need to go back to your manor. You think you're safe here, but you're not."

Nathaniel scoffed, crossing his arms. "And you think my home will offer better protection?"

"In the public eye, yes," she pressed. "There are whispers, Nathaniel. People are saying that your household is weak. That you can't even protect yourself from Ashford."

Evangeline flinched at the words. Nathaniel's expression darkened, his pride stung. His shoulders squared, his jaw tightening as he took a step forward.

"And how exactly do *you* know all of this?" His voice was

razor-sharp. "How do you know so much about my life? Where I am? Who I'm with?"

Vivianne's gaze darted away, her entire body trembling. "I..."

"Vivianne." His voice was low, dangerous. "Tell me the truth."

Her lips parted, then shut again, as if she couldn't force the words out. Finally, she exhaled shakily, meeting his gaze. "Because Ashford asked me to spy on you."

Silence.

Evangeline inhaled sharply. Nathaniel's hands curled into fists at his sides.

Vivianne's voice cracked. "At first, it was easy," she admitted, her eyes flickering with shame. "You and I were... together. It wasn't hard to report back. But after you ended things, it became more difficult. I had to find other ways to keep an ear on you."

Nathaniel let out a harsh, humourless laugh. "So all this time, you've been feeding him information?"

Vivianne shook her head vehemently. "Not anymore. At least, nothing of real value. You have to understand—when a duke summons me, I don't have a choice. I have to go," she said, her voice strained. Then, after a brief pause, she added, "Not since the night of Lady Evangeline's engagement ball." Her gaze flickered to Evangeline, raw and desperate. "When you didn't appear that night, I knew something was wrong. And I knew I had to act."

Evangeline's eyes narrowed. "So what?" Her voice was icy. "This is your redemption arc?"

Vivianne's throat bobbed. "I don't expect forgiveness. I don't even deserve it. But I *do* want Ashford gone. And I want to help you do it."

Nathaniel shook his head. "Why now? Why *this* moment?"

Vivianne exhaled shakily, haunted. "Because when I went

to report to Ashford, I saw the forged letter on his desk. The one that was meant to turn you against Nathaniel." She turned to Evangeline, voice cracking. "I knew then that he wasn't going to stop until he had you completely under his control. And I knew as long as he was around, none of us would be free."

Her tone turned bitter. "That night with Nathaniel, when Ashford forced me to spread the rumours—I thought I could survive it. I thought I could keep my head down. But he made me tell the girls, forced them to spread the story to the men they were with, to travellers and merchants. That's how it spread so quickly. He engineered *all* of it."

Evangeline's stomach churned, bile rising in her throat.

Nathaniel's face was stone. "He forced you?"

Vivianne let out a short, broken laugh. "He owned me, Nathaniel. Just as he thinks he owns Evangeline now." She looked between them, voice thick with remorse. "I want him gone. And if helping you is the only way to make that happen, then that's what I'll do."

Nathaniel's jaw clenched. He remained silent for a long moment, his eyes searching Vivianne's face. Then, finally, he exhaled, shaking his head. "You've made a dangerous choice, Vivianne."

"I know."

Evangeline's voice was sharp, but quieter now. "And what do you expect from us?"

Vivianne squared her shoulders. "I expect nothing. But if you'll have me, I'll be your eyes inside Ashford's circle."

A long silence stretched between them.

Finally, Nathaniel nodded. "Then let's end this."

Chapter Fourteen

Ashford arrived at his estate like a storm barely contained, his presence exuding cold, calculated menace. The news of Nathaniel and Evangeline's return had reached him, and his blood simmered beneath his carefully composed exterior. His hands flexed at his sides, his expression unreadable—only the sharp glint in his eyes betrayed his rage.

The grand doors swung open, and Vivianne stepped inside, breathless from the night's journey. Her cloak clung to her damp body, her hair disheveled, and her chest rose and fell in rapid succession. She barely had time to catch her breath before Ashford's voice sliced through the silence.

"Well?" he asked, his tone deathly calm, though the tension in the room thickened like an impending storm.

Vivianne hesitated, knowing there was no way to soften what she had to say. "The assassin is dead."

A single breath passed. Then another.

And then Ashford exploded.

With a sharp, violent motion, he seized the nearest object —a finely crafted chair—and hurled it against the wall. The wood splintered on impact, crashing to the floor in a pile of broken fragments. The sound rang through the vast estate, but the silence that followed was far louder.

Vivianne flinched. She had seen him angry before—many times—but this was something different.

His head snapped toward her, his gaze burning with fury. "*How?*" he demanded, his voice laced with venom.

She swallowed hard. "Nathaniel fought him off. And Evangeline—"

"*Evangeline?*" he spat the name like it was poison. "Are you telling me *she* had a hand in this?"

Vivianne's throat tightened. "She saved him."

Ashford let out a slow exhale, but it did nothing to ease the darkness in his expression. His hand flexed again—this time not around a chair but into a fist. His next words were measured, restrained, but no less menacing. "And when, exactly, were you planning to inform me of all this?"

Vivianne took a step back instinctively. "I— I came as soon as I could."

His lips curled into something akin to a sneer. "Too late."

Before she could react, his hand lashed out, striking her across the face.

Vivianne staggered, her vision blurring for a moment. She barely caught herself before hitting the ground.

"Ashford," she gasped, holding her cheek, her voice laced with terror. "Please, I tried—"

"You *failed*," he hissed. "Had you reported back to me *sooner*, I could have sent more men. I could have caught them off guard. But instead, *you* ensured they had time to prepare. Tell me, Vivianne—do you think I don't see your cowardice? Do you think I don't *know* you hesitated?"

She shook her head desperately. "I swear, I only did what I thought best."

His eyes gleamed with cruel satisfaction at her fear. "Then consider this your burden to bear," he said coldly. "Either you take your punishment, or your girls will suffer tenfold."

Vivianne paled. "No. Not them. Please."

Ashford's hand came down again, harder this time.

Tears blurred her vision, but she forced herself to stay standing, to not crumble beneath his blows. She knew this pain. She had lived it before. But this time, something inside her fought back.

This will end.

As he raised his hand once more, she clenched her jaw, swallowing the sob that threatened to escape.

I will make sure of it.

Nathaniel and Evangeline sat in the quiet of his study, the tension between them palpable. A single candle flickered beside them, its glow casting long shadows against the walls.

Evangeline's hands tightened in her lap. "People will start talking again," she murmured. "About me. About us."

Nathaniel exhaled sharply, his expression unreadable.

"I will have to live a life of scandal once again," she continued, her voice bitter. "A life I tried so desperately to escape."

She knew what would come. The whispers behind lace fans, the pointed stares, the endless gossip in the drawing rooms of the ton.

Nathaniel's jaw clenched. "Then we make our own arrangement."

Evangeline looked at him sharply. "What are you saying?"

Nathaniel turned to her fully, his voice steady, unwavering.

"Marry me," he said. "And you will be free from his claim."

Evangeline gasped, her heart stuttering in her chest.

His gaze bore into hers, filled with something fierce, something resolute.

"This is the only way," he continued. "If you end your engagement in public, in front of witnesses, Ashford will have no hold over you. And if you become my wife, no one will question why you are with me."

Evangeline swallowed hard, her mind reeling. "Nathaniel, this is—"

"Necessary," he interrupted. "This is the way we end this. The way we take back control."

She searched his face, looking for hesitation, for doubt, but found none.

Slowly, she exhaled.

"Then we confront Ashford."

A sharp knock echoed through the halls of Nathaniel's estate. The servants, recognising the urgency in the visitor's expression, wasted no time in guiding her toward Nathaniel's chambers.

Nathaniel, seated at the edge of his desk, barely looked up from the map he had been studying. "Tell them to wait," he murmured distractedly.

The maid hesitated before stepping forward. "My lord, she says it is urgent. She must see you now."

Eva, who had been seated nearby, arched a brow. "Who is it?"

Before the maid could answer, Vivianne stepped inside.

Lip split. Face pale. Shoulders trembling.

Their hearts sank at the sight of her.

Nathaniel pushed to his feet, his expression hardening. "What happened to you?"

Vivianne exhaled shakily, lowering her gaze. "Ashford. He... he blames me for the assassin's failure. He took it out on me. And if I return, it won't just be me who suffers—my girls... they will pay for my mistakes."

Eva had spent months despising Vivianne, unable to stand the sight of her. The bitterness, the betrayal—it all had left a wound too deep to ignore. But now, seeing her like this, bruised and shaking, she realised something with unsettling clarity: Vivianne had been just as much a pawn in this as she had. Ashford had orchestrated all of it, twisting their lives into something cruel and inescapable.

She clenched her fists, fury surging through her veins. "Then we end this. Once and for all."

Vivianne's eyes pleaded. "Please, Eva. If you truly want to destroy him, return to him. Make him believe you're his. You'll have more power that way."

But Eva shook her head, determination blazing in her eyes. "There's no need. Nathaniel and I are to be wed. Ashford is no longer a problem."

Vivianne's breath hitched. "You're... engaged?"

Eva lifted her chin. "Yes. And that means I am no longer bound to that man. He has no claim over me."

Vivianne swallowed hard, nodding slowly. "Then strike now. Tonight. One of his cousins is hosting a ball. Ashford will be there."

Nathaniel met Eva's gaze, reading the unspoken agreement between them. The time had come.

Vivianne straightened, brushing damp strands of hair from her face. "Then I will ensure he doesn't see you coming."

She turned on her heel, leaving them in heavy silence.

Nathaniel inhaled deeply. "We confront him tonight. No more games."

Eva nodded. "No more games."

Nathaniel stood at the base of the grand staircase, adjusting the cuffs of his dark coat, his fingers tightening as he glanced toward the landing above. He was ready—his sword strapped to his waist, his mind sharpened with anticipation. But for once, he found himself impatient for something beyond the coming fight.

His breath caught as Evangeline stepped into view.

The world seemed to slow.

She was radiant, draped in a gown of deep sapphire blue, the fabric shimmering under the glow of the chandeliers. The cut of the dress was daring yet regal, accentuating every elegant curve. Pearls glistened at her throat, but it was her eyes—fierce, determined—that held him captive.

Nathaniel had always found her beautiful, but tonight, she was *devastating*. A force of nature, breathtaking and untouchable.

His hands clenched at his sides, as if resisting the urge to reach for her, to claim her in front of the world. Instead, he swallowed hard and forced a smirk.

"If you were meant to slay me, my love, you've succeeded."

Evangeline descended the stairs slowly, her lips curling. "Then it's a shame that's not tonight's mission."

His chest tightened with something dangerously close to love.

She reached him, and he extended his arm. She slipped her hand into the crook of his elbow, and they moved as one toward the waiting carriage. Their path was set.

The grand hall of Lord Pembroke's estate glittered with opulence, laughter, and the clinking of crystal glasses. The ball was already in full swing when they arrived, stepping through the gilded doors arm in arm.

Whispers ignited like wildfire.

Evangeline could feel the weight of a hundred gazes upon them—her appearance at Nathaniel's side was a scandal in itself, but the way she *looked* at him?

Unforgivable.

She had never gazed at Ashford with such light in her eyes, had never leaned into his touch with such effortless comfort. Nathaniel bent his head slightly to murmur something in her ear, and she laughed—genuinely, without force.

Across the room, Ashford watched.

His fingers tightened around the stem of his champagne glass, his knuckles whitening.

She had never *looked* at him like that. Not once.

Rage coiled in his chest like a living thing, feeding off the sight of her pressed to Nathaniel's side, her head tilting toward him as if they were sharing the most delicious secret. The heat of jealousy burned through him, searing away his composure.

And then, his anger found a target.

With deliberate ease, Ashford raised his glass and struck it lightly with a silver utensil.

The room silenced instantly.

"My esteemed guests," he began, his voice carrying effortlessly through the hall. "Tonight, we gather in celebration. But, it seems, there is *another* cause for amusement."

Nathaniel's body tensed beside Evangeline. She felt it through their joined hands, but before she could speak, Ashford continued.

"It seems our dear Lady Evangeline has had quite the journey, hasn't she?"

He reached into his pocket and unfolded a letter.

The letter.

Evangeline's stomach dropped.

Nathaniel's expression darkened, his hand drifting toward his sword hilt.

Ashford smiled, the picture of cruel amusement. "Shall I read it aloud?" He gave no one time to answer. "'Dearest Vivianne,'" he began mockingly. "'I do not love Evangeline. She was always a means to an end. My heart, my devotion, belongs only to you. The rest of it has been an elaborate game.'"

A hush fell over the room. Murmurs began to ripple through the crowd.

Ashford let the letter fall slightly, watching Evangeline's face. "Well," he mused. "Maybe you are just a common whore after all."

The insult cracked through the air like a whip.

Gasps erupted, but before the sound could fully settle, there was a sharp *shing*—the unmistakable sound of steel leaving its sheath.

Nathaniel's sword was drawn, the tip of the blade pointing directly at Ashford's throat.

"Take it back," Nathaniel growled, his voice a lethal promise.

Ashford laughed. *Laughed.*

The sound was rich with mockery, his head tilting slightly as if this were all a game. "Why should I? The letter speaks for itself."

Chaos erupted.

Nathaniel's men surged forward, met instantly by Ashford's guards. Swords clashed, tables overturned, and the grand, polished floors of Lord Pembroke's estate became a battlefield.

Evangeline stepped back instinctively, watching the mayhem unfold, heart pounding. She barely registered the shouts of noblemen and women fleeing for safety, their dresses and suits dragging in their haste.

She only had eyes for *them.*

Nathaniel and Ashford.

The fighting slowed as the two men circled each other, the remnants of the battle forming a broken ring around them. Bloodied and panting men stood back, watching, as if even they knew this was how it had always meant to end.

Ashford's lip curled. "You cannot kill me in front of all these people."

Nathaniel exhaled sharply. "Why? Afraid of meeting your end in the same dishonour you've dealt to everyone else?"

Ashford smirked. "No. Afraid you'll prove me right."

And then, his gaze slid to Evangeline.

"You love the thrill of the danger, don't you?" he murmured, voice laced with knowing. "You *crave* the power I offer."

The words slithered over her skin, wrapping around something dark and restless inside her.

Because there was truth in them.

She had *thrived* in her defiance. Had savoured the control she had stolen back piece by piece.

For a moment, the world wavered.

But then—

Nathaniel's voice cut through the fog, raw and unshakable.

"She never belonged to you. And she never will."

Evangeline blinked, the haze shattering, and the moment was gone.

Nathaniel's sword pressed against Ashford's throat. *One movement* and it would be over.

But Ashford...

Ashford only smiled.

The air in the grand hall was thick with tension, the scent of overturned champagne and candle smoke mingling with something more primal—fear. All eyes were on Nathaniel and Ashford, two men standing on opposite sides of fate, the blade at Ashford's throat promising bloodshed.

Then, Evangeline stepped forward.

She felt the weight of a hundred stares, felt the eyes of lords and ladies who had whispered about her, who had judged her, who had pitied her. But none of it mattered.

Not anymore.

Her voice, when it came, was quiet but sharp. "You speak of dishonour, Ashford, as though you are not its very embodiment. You stand before these people and spit venom at me, hoping they will not see the filth dripping from your own hands."

Ashford's jaw tensed, his lips curling into something dangerously close to amusement. "Careful, darling. I would hate for you to embarrass yourself any further."

Evangeline let out a short, cold laugh. "Embarrass myself? No, my lord. I am done hiding. If disgrace is to be my fate, let me claim it. But I will not fall alone."

The murmurs grew, uncertain and intrigued.

Evangeline took another step forward, the fire in her veins pushing her forward, demanding she be heard. She turned her gaze to the crowd. "You want a scandal? Then allow me to provide one. You all know Lord Ashford as a man of influence, a man of status. A man who walks among you as though he is untouchable." Her voice dropped, laced with steel. "But let me tell you who he really is."

A hush fell over the room.

Evangeline turned her piercing stare back to Ashford. "You claim I am nothing more than a common whore? Then tell me, my lord, what does that make the women you've used and discarded? The ones you've broken, the ones you've kept under your heel?" Her gaze flickered to the watching nobles. "Shall I name them? Shall I tell their stories? Shall I tell you of Vivianne?"

Ashford's expression flickered—just for a moment—but she saw it. Saw the tension in his shoulders, the anger barely leashed beneath the surface.

She smiled. *Got you.*

"Shall I tell you how he took from her more than what was his to take? How he forced her to whisper his wicked lies in the ears of men, how he made her a pawn in his twisted game?" She tilted her head. "Or shall I speak of his cruelty? Of how he treats those who serve him? How he treats women who dare to think they belong to themselves?"

The murmurs turned into gasps as she reached for the ribbon at her shoulder.

"You would paint me as something shameful, Ashford? Then let them see the truth of *you*."

With a sharp tug, she lowered the edge of her gown, just enough for the room to see. Gasps rippled through the hall as the bruises along her collarbone and shoulder came into view —faint, but unmistakable. Evidence of his violence. Evidence of who he truly was.

A noblewoman's voice cut through the silence. "Gods above..."

Ashford took a step toward her, his face twisting with something wild. "Enough."

But she did not falter.

She straightened her spine, voice ringing through the hall like a bell of reckoning. "No, my lord. It is *not* enough. It will never be enough. I will not cower in your shadow. I will not let you twist my name into ruin while yours remains untarnished."

Ashford's hand clenched at his side, but the weight of the crowd had shifted. The tide had turned. The murmurs had become whispers of *disgust,* of *condemnation.*

He knew it. And so did she.

Nathaniel, his sword still poised at Ashford's throat, exhaled a slow breath. His voice, when it came, was rough and filled with quiet pride. "You have lost, Ashford."

Ashford's lip curled, his composure fracturing. "You think this ends here?"

Evangeline's voice was softer now, almost pitying. "I think your reign of control ends tonight."

Silence stretched between them, thick and unyielding.

And then, in the flickering candlelight of the grand hall, Ashford laughed.

But it was hollow.

Because he knew.

He had already lost.

Evangeline stood firm, her blood roaring in her ears, the weight of the entire room pressing down upon her. But she did not waver. Not now. Not ever again.

Her voice, though steady, rang out like a war drum, relentless and unyielding.

"And this is just the beginning of your sins, Ashford. I wonder, shall I speak of your forged letters next?" She tilted her head, the fire in her gaze unwavering. "Shall I tell these fine people how you sat behind your grand desk, quill in hand, writing falsehoods to tarnish Lord Sinclair's honor? How you spun deceit to make me doubt the man who has risked his life —*his very soul*—for my safety?"

The murmurs in the crowd grew louder.

Ashford's expression twisted, but before he could speak, Evangeline stepped forward.

"Do not interrupt me," she snapped, her voice cutting like a whip. "I have been silent for *too long*."

Nathaniel, still holding his blade at Ashford's throat, barely contained his smirk. Gods, how he adored her.

Evangeline pressed on, relentless. "Shall I tell them how you sent a man into the night with orders to slit Nathaniel's throat? How you cowered in the shadows while others dirtied their hands with your schemes?"

Gasps erupted around the ballroom.

"Or, perhaps," Evangeline's voice lowered, sharp as a dagger, "I should tell them about the night we fled London. How Nathaniel, a *true* nobleman, dragged me through the darkness, always shielding me, because *he* feared for my life more than his own." She turned her gaze back to Ashford, watching the fury brewing in his features. "How he knew you were watching us, spying on us like a deranged spectre, waiting for the moment to strike. *Like a coward.*"

The crowd shifted—expressions of unease, nobles whispering, eyes darting between Ashford and Nathaniel.

Evangeline inhaled sharply, shaking her head. "I would call you a madman, Ashford, but that would imply you have passion. No, you are something much worse. You are a man who *thinks* himself powerful, but in truth, you are nothing more than a parasite."

Ashford's hand clenched into a fist. "You dare—"

"*I dare!*" she roared, taking another step forward. "You would have stolen my freedom, my future, my *very breath*, and for what? Because you could not bear to lose control? Because a woman standing beyond your grasp made you feel *small*?" She exhaled sharply, every word striking with deadly precision.

"You sent a man to *kill* Nathaniel. Kill the love of my life! And when that failed, you resorted to cowardice. To deceit. To manipulation. And now, with every desperate moment, you are unraveling before us all."

Silence filled the room. The weight of her words crushed everything else beneath them.

And then, Evangeline's voice softened—but it was no less dangerous.

"And let me be clear," she whispered, her eyes never leaving Ashford's. "If Vivianne is harmed in any way—*any* way—understand that you are not just offending her. You are offending Lord Sinclair's household. And that, Ashford, is an act of *war*."

Nathaniel felt a rush of pride so fierce, so overwhelming, he could scarcely contain it. *The love of my life.* She had said it. Declared it for all to hear. He wanted to seize her right then, to kiss her, to tell her he had never loved her more—but he settled for gripping his sword just a little tighter, his heart thundering in his chest.

Ashford, however, trembled with rage. His face was livid, veins bulging at his temples. "This is heresy! Lies spun by a *woman* who has thrown herself into disgrace!"

Evangeline arched a brow. "Then prove me wrong, my lord. Deny it before all these people. But be warned—they have seen the bruises on my skin. They have heard the venom in your words. And I dare say—" she glanced at the gathering nobles, whose disgusted murmurs were growing louder by the second—"they will not be so eager to believe you anymore."

Ashford's fists clenched, his breathing labored. *He was cornered.*

So, he did what desperate men always did.

He lashed out.

A bitter sneer twisted Ashford's face as he took a step closer. "And you think Nathaniel is any better? You think he is some noble hero?" He laughed, the sound laced with venom.

"He is no better than me, Evangeline. He plays the part well, I'll admit, but he is cut from the same cloth as every man in this room. He takes what he wants, without a care for the consequences."

Nathaniel scoffed. "That's rich, coming from a man who relies on deception and threats to wield power. I've never needed to trap a woman in a cage to feel powerful."

Ashford's gaze darkened. "You think yourself her saviour? Her protector? Spare me. You didn't fight for her when it mattered. You *let* her fall. And now you come crawling back, hoping to mend what was never yours to begin with."

Nathaniel's jaw clenched, rage simmering beneath the surface. "I made mistakes. But I have never, *never* sought to own her. She is with me because she chooses to be. That is something you will never understand."

Ashford laughed coldly. "Ah, and what a beautiful tale that is. The noble knight and his lady, bound by fate. But tell me, Lord Sinclair—if she had nowhere else to run, would you still call it love? Or would you call it desperation?"

Nathaniel's patience snapped. "Enough. You have dishonoured me before all of society," he spat. "And for that, I demand satisfaction."

The air thickened.

A duel.

Nathaniel's lips curled into something feral, something *thrilled.*

"Name your time and place," he said, his voice like steel.

Ashford's gaze burned with hatred. "Five days from now. At dawn."

Nathaniel grinned. "I'll be waiting."

A collective gasp rang through the hall.

Evangeline exhaled, knowing the storm had only begun.

The ride home was silent, the weight of the night pressing upon them both. Evangeline's hands were folded in her lap, her knuckles white. Nathaniel stole glances at her from across the carriage, knowing that her mind was far from still.

When they arrived, the moment their feet touched the polished floors of Nathaniel's estate, he turned to her with a small, knowing smile.

"You know," he murmured, removing his gloves, "I had every intention of announcing our engagement tonight."

Evangeline's eyes flickered to him, unreadable.

Nathaniel took a slow step closer. "But then you stood there, so masterful, so unshaken. You commanded the entire room, exposed that wretch for what he was. I fell in love with your bravery all over again."

Evangeline exhaled sharply, looking away. "Nathaniel..."

"Don't," he said softly. "Don't retreat from me now."

She whirled on him, anger flashing across her features. "How can you speak of love so easily? Do you not understand that I may lose you in five days?!" Her voice cracked, and she hated the way the words made her feel exposed, weak.

Nathaniel's smile faded, replaced with something far more solemn. "You won't."

She let out a short, bitter laugh. "You say that as if it is fact. But this is a duel, Nathaniel. It is not some drunken tavern brawl. There are rules—honor and blood. You *could*—"

"I won't." His tone was firm, unwavering.

Evangeline clenched her fists. "I do not want the *possibility* of losing you. Do you understand that? If you die, what then? Am I supposed to just... go on? Marry another? Live with the weight of knowing that the man I love died because of *me*?"

Nathaniel's breath hitched at her words, but she was too consumed by her anger, by her fear, to notice.

"Do you think I *want* to risk my life?" he said, his voice gentler now. "Do you think I would put myself in harm's way if there was another way? If I could rid us of Ashford without taking up a sword, I would. But I *must* see this through. Not just for me. For you. For Vivianne. For every soul that wretch has ever laid his hands upon."

Evangeline looked at him, her eyes shining with fury and something dangerously close to love. "Then promise me. Promise me that you will survive. That you will come back to me."

Nathaniel reached for her then, cupping her face between his hands. "I swear to you, Evangeline. I will not leave you. I will win. And when I do, I will spend every remaining day of my life proving to you that you were worth fighting for."

Her lips parted, but no words came. Instead, she closed her eyes, leaning into his touch, breathing in the scent of him, letting his warmth soothe the storm inside her.

For now, it would have to be enough.

Chapter Fifteen

The morning sun crept over the horizon, casting long golden streaks across the dewy lawn of Nathaniel's estate. The grounds, usually alive with the movements of staff, felt still, as if the air itself was holding its breath in anticipation. The duel was mere hours away, and for the first time in years, Evangeline felt powerless.

She stood on the terrace, arms wrapped around herself, her eyes locked on the two figures in the training yard below. Nathaniel moved with measured precision, his sword slicing through the cool morning air as he parried an incoming strike. His opponent—a broad-shouldered man with greying hair and a face worn by years of combat—pressed forward, testing Nathaniel's defences.

"You need to stop hesitating on your right side," the older man barked, disengaging and stepping back. "If he's watched you fight before, he'll exploit it."

Nathaniel exhaled sharply, rolling his shoulders. "He fights like a man who has never had to earn his victories," he replied. "He'll go for my wounded side first. He won't fight fair."

The trainer scoffed. "Then why the hell are you fighting fair?"

Nathaniel shot him a warning glance. "Because I am not him."

From the terrace, Evangeline felt a sharp pang in her chest. Nathaniel spoke with conviction, but she saw the tension in his frame, the rigid way he held himself. He wasn't just fighting for honor—he was fighting for something far more personal. For her. For justice. And yet, she couldn't shake the fear that he might not walk away from this.

The older man wiped his brow and lowered his sword. "You've got strength, Sinclair. More than him. But strength isn't everything. What happens if you get him on his knees? Will you finish it?"

A silence fell between them. Nathaniel hesitated just long enough for Evangeline's stomach to twist.

"I haven't decided yet," Nathaniel admitted, his voice quieter now.

The trainer sighed. "Decide before you step onto that field. Hesitation gets men killed."

The air in Evangeline's chambers was thick with tension, the morning light barely filtering through the heavy drapes. Evangeline gripped the terrace railing, her breath uneven. This wasn't just a duel. It was a battle for everything. And she wasn't sure if she could bear to watch it unfold.

Evangeline stood by the window, her arms crossed tightly over her chest, watching the courtyard below. Nathaniel was already there, stripped to his waist, sword in hand, moving through the motions of his training. The rhythmic sound of steel slicing through the air filled the quiet space, but it did nothing to calm the storm within her.

She hated watching him like this. Hated seeing him prepare for a fight that could take him away from her forever.

Each swing of his blade felt like a countdown, every measured movement a reminder that in just a few days, he would stand before Ashford with nothing but his skill and honor to protect him. And if he lost—

No.

Evangeline clenched her hands into fists. She would not allow that thought to take root.

"My lady, you should not be watching this," came the quiet voice of her maid, Elise, from behind her.

Evangeline didn't turn. "Then what should I be doing? Sitting idly by while Nathaniel risks his life?"

Elise hesitated before stepping closer. "You should be preparing for the possibility that he does not return."

The words struck like a blow. Evangeline spun to face her, her eyes flashing. "How dare you—"

"I speak only the truth, my lady," Elise interrupted gently but firmly. "He is a nobleman, yes, but he is still a man. And men die in duels. Especially against men like Ashford."

Evangeline opened her mouth to argue, to rebuke the thought outright, but the words caught in her throat. She had spent days suppressing the very same fear. Hearing it spoken aloud made it all the more real.

"You do not understand," Evangeline murmured, turning back to the window, her voice quieter now. "Nathaniel is not just any man."

Elise sighed, stepping beside her. "Then tell me, my lady. How did you first know? That he was different?"

Evangeline's breath caught as memories flooded her mind—memories of a time before scandal, before betrayal, before everything had unraveled.

It had been at a summer ball, years ago. She had been fresh-faced, still naïve to the politics of society. The room had been alight with candle chandeliers, the air thick with perfume and laughter. She had danced with suitors all evening, exchanging pleasantries, making careful conversation. And then she had seen *him*.

Nathaniel had stood apart from the crowd, leaning against the far column, a glass of wine in hand, watching the room with an amused smirk. He had been effortless in his confidence, exuding a quiet power that made her breath hitch. But it was not his looks or his charm that had drawn her in—it was the moment their eyes met across the room.

There had been something in his gaze. A challenge. A recognition.

And then, when he finally approached her, his first words had not been some flowery praise or an attempt at flattery. No. He had smirked and said, *"Are you always this charming, or is it just for the benefit of your audience?"*

She had been speechless for the first time in her life.

Evangeline let out a shaky breath, returning to the present. "I knew the moment he first looked at me that he was going to change everything. And he did."

Elise watched her carefully. "And now?"

Evangeline swallowed hard. "Now, I fear he will change everything again. But this time... by leaving me behind."

For the first time, Evangeline allowed a tear to slip down her cheek. Elise said nothing, only reaching out and placing a steadying hand on her shoulder. They stood together in silence, watching Nathaniel train below, both knowing that no words could soothe what was to come.

The library was dimly lit, the golden glow of candlelight flickering off the spines of books that lined the walls. Evangeline sat curled in one of the high-backed chairs, a book resting open in her lap though she had long since given up on reading.

She heard his footsteps before she saw him.

Nathaniel entered quietly, his presence filling the space as he leaned against the doorframe. "You disappeared on me."

She didn't look up. "I needed a moment."

He exhaled softly, crossing the room and lowering himself into the chair opposite hers. "You're angry."

Evangeline snapped the book shut and finally met his gaze. "Of course I am. You are being reckless, Nathaniel. You know Ashford will not fight fair. And yet, you refuse to take any precautions beyond your own strength."

Nathaniel studied her, his expression unreadable. "You think I have not considered every move he might make? That I have not planned for every possible outcome?"

"I think you are too willing to trust that honor will prevail," she countered, her voice sharp. "And honor does not win against men like him."

A long silence stretched between them. Then, slowly, Nathaniel reached into the pocket of his waistcoat and withdrew a small object, rolling it between his fingers before extending it to her.

Evangeline hesitated before reaching out, her breath catching as she saw what it was—a pendant, simple yet elegant, the metal warm from his touch. The crest of his family was engraved in the center, a mark of legacy and promise.

"No matter what happens," he murmured, "I will always belong to you."

Her fingers curled around the pendant, her throat tightening. "You cannot promise that."

Nathaniel leaned forward, his voice steady. "But I can promise that I will fight like a man who has something worth coming back for."

Evangeline exhaled sharply, looking down at the pendant in her palm. "And if you don't? If he wins?"

Nathaniel reached out, tilting her chin so that their eyes met. "Then know that I fought for you until my last breath. But I am not planning to lose, Evangeline. Not to him. Not now."

She shook her head. "You're too confident. That is what worries me."

He let out a soft chuckle, though there was no humour in it. "And you worry too much. That is what worries *me*."

Evangeline clutched the pendant against her chest, closing her eyes for a brief moment. "Swear to me, Nathaniel. Swear to me that you will come back."

His expression turned solemn as he leaned in closer, his

forehead brushing against hers. "I swear that I will do everything in my power to return to you. But you must swear something to me in return."

Her breath hitched. "What?"

Nathaniel's fingers trailed lightly over her hand. "That if I do come back, you will no longer run from me."

A long pause stretched between them, filled with silent, heavy understanding.

Evangeline finally whispered, "Then I swear it."

Nathaniel kissed her forehead softly, lingering just a moment longer. "Then we both have something to fight for."

For the first time in days, Evangeline felt something other than fear.

The evening before the duel settled over the estate like a heavy shroud. The corridors of the house, usually buzzing with the quiet hum of conversation and the shuffle of servants, were eerily subdued. Candlelight flickered against the polished wood of the grand hall, throwing elongated shadows that stretched unnervingly along the walls.

Evangeline wandered through the dimly lit corridors, her arms wrapped around herself as if warding off a chill that had nothing to do with the temperature. A hush had fallen over the household, a silence thick with anticipation and unspoken fears. Even the servants, who were rarely afforded the luxury of standing still, moved with an uncharacteristic quiet.

She slowed her steps as she neared the kitchens, the faint murmur of hushed voices drawing her attention. She paused just outside the doorway, careful not to make a sound.

"He's a fine swordsman, no doubt," one voice whispered, low and uncertain. "But Ashford doesn't fight fair. Everyone knows it."

A second voice scoffed. "Does it matter? Sinclair has more honor in his little finger than that snake ever will. I'd place my coin on him."

"Honor doesn't win duels," the first voice countered

grimly. "Skill does. And Ashford's men have been lurking near the estate. Makes you wonder, doesn't it?"

Evangeline's breath hitched. She pressed herself closer to the wall, her heartbeat hammering against her ribs.

"Lurking?" the second voice asked, suddenly wary. "Why?"

"No one knows," the first whispered. "But if Ashford were to try something, now would be the time."

"You mean—before the duel? That'd be madness. Even for him."

"Would it?" the first voice said. "Think about it—if Sinclair doesn't show up tomorrow, the duel never happens. Ashford walks away unchallenged. The scandal fades, and he's still a duke. If he wanted to be rid of Sinclair without lifting a sword, he wouldn't have to try very hard."

A silence stretched between them, and Evangeline could practically hear the weight of their thoughts hanging in the air.

"That's not the worst of it," the second voice finally muttered. "Some of the stable boys said they saw a pair of riders by the back gate just before dusk. They didn't come in. Just... watched. And then they were gone."

Evangeline felt a chill crawl up her spine.

She stepped back from the doorway, her mind racing. If Ashford's men had been seen near the estate, what were they planning? Was the duel truly to be the battle Nathaniel believed it to be—or was there something far more sinister lurking beneath the surface? Was Ashford planning something underhanded? A more permanent solution to his problems?

Her fingers curled into fists. She had spent too much time feeling powerless, too much time watching as Nathaniel placed himself in danger for the sake of honor. But if there was one thing she knew, it was that Ashford didn't deserve the privilege of an honourable fight.

As she turned to leave, the kitchen door suddenly creaked open. Evangeline barely had time to compose herself before one of the maids gasped upon seeing her standing there.

"My lady! I—I didn't know you were—"

Evangeline lifted a hand, silencing her. "What you said just now—about Ashford's men lurking near the estate—how certain are you?"

The two maids exchanged glances, looking nervous. "We only overheard what the stable boys said, my lady. But... it isn't the first time someone's mentioned strange riders near the property."

Evangeline inhaled sharply. "If you hear anything else, anything at all, you will come directly to me. Do you understand?"

They both nodded quickly, eyes wide. "Yes, my lady. Of course."

Without another word, Evangeline turned and hurried back toward her chambers, her mind buzzing with unease. The storm was coming. And she feared they weren't ready for it.

The fire in Nathaniel's room burned low, casting flickering shadows that danced across the dark wood-panelled walls. The weight of the coming dawn pressed heavily upon them both.

Evangeline stood by the door, her fingers gripping the frame as if steadying herself before she spoke. "Nathaniel," she whispered, her voice fragile in the thick silence.

He was seated near the hearth, his shirt half undone, the tension in his shoulders betraying the calm he was trying to maintain. He didn't look up immediately, merely swirling the glass of brandy in his hand before taking a slow sip. "You should be asleep, Evangeline."

She ignored the gentle dismissal and took a step forward. "Come away with me. Now."

Nathaniel froze for the briefest of moments before setting his glass down with deliberate care. Then he turned to look at her, his expression unreadable. "You know I cannot do that."

Evangeline's throat tightened. "Why not? What is keeping you here that is more important than your life? Than *our* life?"

He exhaled sharply and stood, crossing the space between them in three slow strides. "My honor, Evangeline."

She let out a bitter laugh, shaking her head. "Honor? Do you truly believe honor is worth dying for? That a meaningless duel with a man who has already lost in every way that matters is what will make you whole?" She stepped closer, her hands trembling as she reached for him. "You don't have to do this. We can leave tonight. We can start over. We can be free."

Nathaniel caught her hands gently, holding them between his own. "And what then?" he asked softly. "Would you truly be able to live a life knowing we ran from this? That we let him win? That Ashford still walks free, still holds power, still believes he owns everything—including you?"

Evangeline flinched at his words. She knew he was right. And yet, the fear clawing at her insides was relentless. "I don't care about any of that. I only care about you. About waking up tomorrow and knowing you're still alive."

Nathaniel smiled then, but it was a sad, weary thing. He reached up, brushing a loose strand of hair from her face. "You ask me to run, but you would never forgive me if I did."

She inhaled sharply, but before she could protest, he continued, his voice softer now. "If I run, I am no longer the man you love. And you know it."

Evangeline clenched her jaw, shaking her head in frustration. "I love you, you fool. Do you not understand? This isn't about pride. I just want you safe."

Nathaniel let out a breath, his hands tightening slightly around hers. "And I want *you* safe. I cannot protect you if I run, Evangeline. I cannot look at myself in the mirror knowing I let a man like Ashford walk free when I had the power to stop him."

Her eyes burned. "And what if he wins? What if I lose you? What then, Nathaniel? What am I supposed to do?"

He swallowed hard, and for the first time, his composure faltered. He cupped her face, his thumb tracing along her cheekbone. "You will live, Evangeline. You will be strong. And you will remember that I loved you with every piece of me."

She let out a quiet sob, gripping the fabric of his shirt. "I don't want memories. I want *you*."

Nathaniel's own breath shook as he pressed his forehead against hers. "Then wait for me."

"Swear it," she whispered, voice barely audible. "Swear that you will come back. That you will not let him—" She choked on the thought, unable to finish.

Nathaniel pressed a kiss to her forehead, his lips lingering. "I swear that I will fight with everything I have. That I will not fall easily. That I will return to you."

It was not the promise she wanted. But it was the only one he could give her.

She nodded, letting out a shuddering breath. Then, before she could think, before she could let reason stop her, she surged forward and kissed him.

It was not gentle, not tender—it was desperate, raw, filled with the fear of losing him and the agony of knowing she could do nothing to stop it. He kissed her back just as fiercely, as if trying to memorize her, as if this might be their last moment together.

When they finally broke apart, both breathless, she rested her forehead against his. "I love you," she murmured. "I will always love you."

Nathaniel exhaled slowly, his lips brushing against her temple. "Then wait for me."

She closed her eyes, knowing she had no other choice.

The fire crackled, the shadows deepened, and the night crept on toward the dawn that would decide everything.

Chapter Sixteen

The candlelight in Ashford's study flickered against the dark wood-panelled walls, the scent of brandy and cigar smoke thick in the air. The heavy drapes had been drawn shut, drowning the room in a suffocating stillness, save for the occasional crackling of the fire in the hearth.

Ashford sat behind his mahogany desk, fingers drumming lazily against the polished surface. Across from him stood a man cloaked in shadows, his stance relaxed but purposeful. The assassin's presence exuded quiet menace, his cold, calculating eyes scanning the room before settling on Ashford with a practiced indifference.

"You have options," the assassin said, his voice smooth, devoid of emotion. "A carriage accident is simple—swift, tragic, and nearly impossible to trace. Poison would ensure a clean execution, perhaps laced into wine at a dinner, or a slow-working venom that mimics illness. Or—"

He paused, a smirk curling at the corner of his mouth.

"Or, my lord, if you prefer something more... *personal*, there are ways to make it hurt. To make her beg."

Ashford leaned forward, a dark amusement flickering in his gaze. "Tell me."

The assassin's smirk remained. "A staged break-in. A struggle. Fear before death. If you desire, she can suffer long enough to regret every decision that led her to defy you. I can ensure she sees the end coming."

Ashford exhaled, rolling the idea over in his mind like fine wine on his tongue. The image of Evangeline's face—her defiance, her arrogance—flashed in his mind. He thought of the way she had looked at Sinclair, of the way she had clung to him, as if he were something more than a man who would ultimately fail her.

"How long can you make her last?" Ashford asked, swirling the brandy in his glass.

The assassin chuckled. "That depends on how much you want her to suffer. If you want an example, I can make arrangements."

Ashford's lips curled. "No need. Just make it clear. Make her wish she had chosen differently."

"And Sinclair?" the assassin asked. "He will come after you for this."

Ashford leaned back in his chair, eyes cold. "Let him. I want him to know what happens when he takes what belongs to me."

The assassin inclined his head. "As you wish."

Ashford's grip tightened around the glass of brandy in his hand. *By the time Nathaniel Sinclair finds her, there will be nothing left to save.*

The hidden tavern was tucked away in one of London's less reputable alleys, its entrance nearly invisible between the looming brick buildings. Inside, the air was thick with the scent of stale ale, tobacco, and desperation. The dim candlelight barely illuminated the faces of its patrons, most of whom were too engrossed in their own secrets to pay much mind to a lone woman sitting in the farthest corner of the room.

Vivianne sat stiffly, her hood pulled low over her face, her fingers curling and uncurling around the edge of her cloak. She had sent word to Nathaniel, praying he would come.

And now, he had.

Nathaniel stepped into the tavern, his presence commanding despite his efforts to move discreetly. His sharp gaze swept across the room, settling on Vivianne. Without hesitation, he strode toward her, boots echoing against the wooden floor.

He sat across from her, posture tense, eyes filled with suspicion. "You'd best have something worthwhile to say. My patience is thin, Vivianne."

Vivianne exhaled sharply, bracing herself. "I do. And you'll want to hear it."

Nathaniel's expression remained unreadable. "Then talk."

She hesitated, then leaned forward, lowering her voice. "Ashford wants her dead. He's done waiting. The assassin has already been chosen, the plan set in motion."

Nathaniel stiffened, his jaw tightening. "How do you know this?"

Vivianne let out a humourless laugh, shaking her head. "Because important men think women are beneath them. They talk when they shouldn't." She met his gaze, her voice quieter now. "You'd be surprised what they reveal when they believe no one is listening."

Nathaniel's hands curled into fists. "Tell me everything."

Vivianne nodded. "Ashford met with the assassin personally. He didn't just order her death—he wants her to suffer first. He's made sure there will be no ties back to him. No proof."

Nathaniel's teeth clenched. His mind raced. He had prepared for a duel, had anticipated Ashford's usual tactics. But this? This was something else entirely. This was an execution.

Vivianne's voice softened, urgent. "You need to act before it's too late. You need to get her out of London."

Nathaniel exhaled slowly, controlling the fury coursing through him. "And why should I trust you? You were in his pocket once."

Vivianne swallowed hard. "Because I was blind before. Because I was complicit in spreading the rumours that ruined her. But I won't stand by while he takes her life. I won't have that blood on my hands."

Nathaniel studied her for a long moment, weighing her words, searching for any hint of deception. He found none.

Finally, he nodded once, decisive. "Then we move tonight."

Vivianne exhaled, relief flickering across her face. "I'll do whatever I can to help. Just don't let him win."

Nathaniel stood, the chair scraping against the wooden floor. "He won't."

He turned sharply, striding toward the door, his mind already calculating their next steps.

Ashford had made his move.

Now, it was Nathaniel's turn.

The estate was unnervingly quiet, the kind of silence that settled before a storm. Midnight draped the manor in darkness, the only light coming from the dimly flickering lanterns outside and the occasional glow of a dying hearth within. The wind carried a chill, rustling the trees just beyond the estate walls, masking the subtle movements of an unwanted guest.

The assassin had already slipped inside. He wasn't waiting.

A faint creak echoed through the empty corridor near Evangeline's chambers. A draft slipped through the hall, carrying with it the scent of damp earth and something sharper—metallic. A window had been left open, or rather, had been forced open. The thin curtain swayed, revealing a single, gloved hand resting on the windowsill.

A shadow detached itself from the darkness. The assassin moved soundlessly, his steps careful, deliberate. His fingers traced the hilt of a dagger strapped to his thigh, his other hand adjusting the thin wire coiled at his belt. This wasn't a job that required haste—it was meant to be *clean, efficient.*

And it had to be tonight.

Not far from the main corridor, in the servant's quarters, another detail had gone unnoticed. A dagger had been stashed beneath the loose floorboards near the back entrance—a telltale sign that someone on the inside had been involved. Someone had let him in.

Nathaniel had barely settled at his desk when something felt *wrong*. A deep unease slithered down his spine, a feeling he had learned long ago *not* to ignore. He glanced toward the window, then back at the door to his study. A candle flickered, throwing strange shadows across the walls.

Then he heard it.

A shift in the floorboards. Light. Nearly imperceptible. But there.

Nathaniel was on his feet in an instant, muscles tensing. His mind raced through possibilities, through every contingency, but the truth settled in quickly and violently.

He's not waiting for me. He's hunting her.

His heart pounded as he reached for his sword, gripping the hilt with practiced ease. Without another breath, he tore through the hall, his pulse a steady, deafening rhythm in his ears.

And then he heard *another* sound.

A door opening—too softly.

A breath—a slow, measured inhale that did not belong.

He wasn't fast enough to warn her.

The assassin had already found Evangeline's room.

The fire in Evangeline's room had burned low, leaving only embers glowing in the hearth. The room was quiet, the stillness punctuated by the occasional whisper of wind rattling the windowpane. She lay in bed, restless, her mind too cluttered to surrender to sleep. A sense of unease crept through her, an unshakable feeling that something was wrong.

She sat up, frowning into the darkness.

Then she heard it—a sound too soft for an ordinary disturbance. A floorboard creaked, deliberate and measured.

Her breath caught. Someone was in the room.

Evangeline's hand darted beneath her pillow, fingers wrapping around the hilt of a small dagger Nathaniel had insisted she keep close. Slowly, she shifted to the edge of the bed, her pulse thudding against her ribs.

The shadows near the window moved.

She barely had time to react before a figure stepped forward—a man cloaked in darkness, his presence exuding an air of cold calculation. The glint of steel in his hand caught the faint light of the dying fire.

"Clever girl," the assassin murmured as she lunged.

Evangeline thrust the dagger forward, aiming for his chest, but he was quicker. He twisted, avoiding a fatal wound, but she felt the blade sink into his arm. He let out a hiss of pain, recoiling slightly, but not enough to slow him down.

Before she could strike again, he caught her wrist and twisted it violently, forcing her to drop the weapon. Pain shot up her arm as she gasped, struggling against his grip.

The assassin chuckled, low and cruel. "You've got fight in you. That'll make this more entertaining."

Evangeline wrenched against his hold, her heart hammering wildly. "You'll regret this," she spat, but fear coiled tight in her stomach.

The man merely smirked. "Ashford wanted me to have some fun first."

Revulsion and terror clashed within her. She kicked out, landing a blow against his leg, but he barely stumbled. His free hand wrapped around her throat, shoving her back against the bedpost.

Then—

A deafening crash.

The door slammed open.

Nathaniel.

He stood in the threshold, chest heaving, eyes ablaze with fury. But he was unarmed.

Evangeline's heart lurched. The assassin tightened his grip, a blade now pressed against her throat.

"One more step, Sinclair, and I'll slit her pretty little throat."

Nathaniel didn't move. Didn't breathe.

Evangeline's mind raced, desperation clawing at her. Nathaniel was staring at her, his hands twitching at his sides. She knew that look—he was waiting for an opening.

She just had to give him one.

The room was suffocating in its silence.

Evangeline could feel the assassin's breath against her skin, the sharp edge of the blade pressing against her throat. One wrong move and it would be over. But she saw it—the flicker in Nathaniel's eyes, the way his hands flexed at his sides. He was waiting. Calculating.

She had to act.

With all the strength she could muster, Evangeline wrenched her body sideways, twisting just enough to throw the assassin off balance. His grip faltered, but the knife sliced across her collarbone—a sharp, burning pain. She barely had time to register it before Nathaniel lunged.

The force of his attack sent both men crashing into the hallway. They hit the wooden floor with a resounding thud, the assassin rolling swiftly to his feet, dagger raised. Nathaniel was already pushing himself up, his body coiled with tension.

But he was unarmed.

The assassin smirked. "You always were too reckless, Sinclair. You should've stayed in your room."

Nathaniel didn't answer. He surged forward, dodging the first slash and catching the assassin's wrist mid-swing. The dagger halted inches from his throat. With a vicious twist,

Nathaniel wrenched the man's arm back, forcing him to drop the blade. It clattered to the floor.

The assassin reacted instantly, slamming his knee into Nathaniel's ribs. The force knocked the air from his lungs, but Nathaniel refused to fall. He swung, landing a brutal punch to the assassin's jaw, sending him staggering back.

Blood dripped from the corner of the assassin's mouth. He wiped it away with the back of his hand, his grin never faltering. "Not bad. But you're bleeding."

Nathaniel's vision blurred for a moment. A hot, wet sensation spread across his side. He looked down to see the thin, glistening line of a fresh wound—a deep gash slicing across his ribs.

Evangeline screamed his name, but he couldn't stop. Wouldn't stop.

The assassin lunged again, faster this time. Nathaniel barely dodged the strike, twisting his body just in time to avoid another fatal wound. His muscles screamed in protest, but he didn't slow.

Then—

A gunshot.

The sharp crack of a pistol shattered the night.

The assassin froze, his body jerking violently. A dark stain blossomed across his chest. He stumbled, his dagger slipping from his grasp before he crumpled to the floor.

Vivianne stood at the end of the hall, a smoking pistol in her shaking hands. Her breath was ragged, her eyes wide with horror. She had never taken a life before.

Nathaniel staggered back, clutching his side as blood seeped through his fingers. He turned to Evangeline, who had rushed to his side, hands pressing against his wound, desperate to stop the bleeding.

The assassin was dead.

But Nathaniel was barely standing.

Chapter Seventeen

Nathaniel slumped into his study chair, his breath ragged, his hand pressing against the wound at his side. Blood stained his shirt, dark and seeping, the price of his battle with the assassin. His body ached, every movement laced with pain, but he refused to succumb to weakness.

Evangeline knelt beside him, her hands shaking as she pressed a cloth against his wound. "You need a physician," she said, her voice unsteady.

Nathaniel let out a low, humourless chuckle. "No time."

"Nathaniel—"

"This isn't a duel anymore," he cut her off, voice raw with barely restrained fury. "This is war."

Evangeline inhaled sharply, her hands pausing against his wound. The man before her was different now—his usual cool, collected demeanour had shattered. He was enraged. And that scared her.

Vivianne stepped forward, her face pale. "It was him," she confirmed, voice barely above a whisper. "Ashford gave the order. He wanted it done before the duel. Before he had to face you."

Nathaniel's grip tightened around the armrest of his chair, his knuckles turning white. "Coward," he spat, his voice laced with venom. "He couldn't kill me himself, so he sent someone to take Evangeline first."

Vivianne swallowed hard. "There's no doubt now. He won't stop. Not until you're both dead."

Evangeline turned to Nathaniel, her eyes searching his. "Then what do we do?" she asked, fear and fury interwoven in her voice.

Nathaniel exhaled slowly, the weight of his next words pressing on him. "We finish this. Once and for all."

Evangeline tightened her grip on his bloodied hand. She had never seen such an unrelenting fire in his eyes before. But she would stand beside him. No matter what came next.

The study was steeped in an eerie stillness, the fire in the hearth reduced to a bed of glowing embers. Outside, dawn had yet to break, the night clinging stubbornly to the sky. The only sound was the slow, deliberate tearing of fabric as Nathaniel wrapped a fresh bandage around his side.

Evangeline sat on the edge of his desk, watching him in silence. The man before her was not the same one she had fallen in love with. This was someone darker, someone shaped by rage and vengeance.

Nathaniel tied the bandage off with a sharp tug, his jaw tight. "He doesn't deserve a fair fight," he said, his voice low and edged with something dangerous. "He doesn't deserve an easy death."

Evangeline shivered at the finality in his tone. "Nathaniel... this isn't just about honor anymore, is it?"

He met her gaze, and for the first time, she saw it—the war raging inside him. The part of him that wanted blood. That *needed* it.

"No," he admitted. "Not anymore."

Evangeline's throat tightened. "You were never this man before. He's turning you into something else."

Nathaniel exhaled through his nose, his eyes like steel. "I promise to do whatever it takes to keep you safe. Whatever it takes."

She flinched at the words, at their weight. "And if it changes you forever? If you become like him?"

He stepped closer, lifting a hand to cup her face. His touch was rougher than usual, his thumb tracing the curve of her cheek. "I would rather be a monster who protects you than a man who watches you die."

Tears burned at the edges of her vision, but she refused to let them fall. "Nathaniel, I don't want to lose you—not like this."

His fingers tightened ever so slightly. "You won't. But I need you to understand... there's no coming back from this. If he wants a war, I'll give him one."

Evangeline's breath hitched. She had spent so long fighting against fate, against the pain of losing him. But now, she realised something more terrifying than loss—

She was watching the man she loved become something else.

Nathaniel's chambers were cloaked in the quiet stillness before dawn. The fire had burned down to embers, casting long shadows across the room. A storm raged inside Evangeline, though she stood frozen at the threshold, her hands clasped tightly in front of her.

He was seated on the edge of the bed, elbows braced on his knees, his head lowered. The flickering candlelight made him look almost ethereal—tired, battle-worn, lost in thought. His shirt was still undone from where she had helped him dress his wound, the white linen marred with traces of dried blood.

Evangeline swallowed hard and stepped forward. "I need you to promise me something."

Nathaniel's gaze lifted, weary but sharp. "Anything."

She hesitated, forcing herself to hold his gaze. "Promise me you'll come back."

A long silence stretched between them, thick with unspoken truths.

Finally, he exhaled. "Evangeline..."

She clenched her fists. "No. No 'but.' No hesitation. Just promise me."

Nathaniel stood, moving toward her with a measured slowness. When he reached her, he lifted a hand, brushing his knuckles against her cheek. "You know I can't."

Tears burned behind her eyes, but she refused to let them fall. "Then what am I supposed to do? Watch you ride off to your death? Pretend this is just another battle, another test of your damn honor?" Her voice cracked. "I can't do it, Nathaniel. I can't lose you."

He sighed, a weary sound, before reaching into his pocket. He pulled out something small—cool metal glinting in the candlelight.

A pendant.

The same one he had given her once before, when things were simpler. When their love had been untouched by betrayal, by war.

He pressed it into her palm, curling her fingers around it. "Then let this be my promise to you. No matter what happens, I will always belong to you."

Evangeline stared at the pendant in her trembling hand. "This isn't enough."

Nathaniel cupped her face, tilting her chin up so she had no choice but to look at him. "Then promise me something in return."

Her breath hitched. "What?"

His gaze darkened, but there was something softer beneath the steel. "If I don't come back, don't let this world break you. Don't let it steal your fire."

A tear slipped down her cheek. "Nathaniel—"

"Promise me, Evangeline."

She let out a shaky breath, then nodded. "I promise."

Nathaniel leaned in, pressing his forehead against hers. "Then that's enough for me."

She closed her eyes, holding onto him, onto this moment, onto the fleeting warmth of his touch, praying it wouldn't be the last.

The chamber was cast in shadows, the candlelight flickering against the stone walls, bathing the room in a golden glow. Outside, the world was silent, the weight of the coming dawn pressing against the still air.

Nathaniel lay beside her, his body warm, solid—a presence that had once felt unshakable, but now seemed so fleeting, so fragile.

They had made love, but it was not the fevered passion of desire. It was desperation. A memorisation of each other. Every touch, every sigh, every whispered name—etched into skin, into breath, into the very marrow of their bones. As if they could hold onto each other forever through the sheer will of their bodies entangled beneath the sheets.

Evangeline pressed her palm against his chest, feeling the steady beat of his heart beneath her fingers. Slow, calm, steady —so different from the turmoil inside her.

Nathaniel exhaled, pressing a soft kiss to her temple. "You're quiet."

She traced a fingertip along a scar near his shoulder, following its path down to the ridge of muscle on his back. "Where did this one come from?"

He chuckled, the sound low and rough. "A duel. Years ago. I was arrogant. Thought I was untouchable. My opponent proved otherwise."

Evangeline frowned, her fingers drifting lower, mapping out another mark, this one along his ribs. "And this?"

Nathaniel's hand covered hers, stopping her exploration. "You don't need to memorize my scars, Evangeline."

She swallowed, her throat tight. "Yes, I do."

He stilled, understanding dawning in his eyes.

"Just in case," she whispered, forcing the words out. "Just in case this is all I have left of you."

Nathaniel rolled onto his side, framing her face between his hands. "Look at me."

She did. And what she saw nearly shattered her. There was no fear in his gaze, no uncertainty—only love, deep and unwavering.

"You will have more than memories of me, Evangeline. I swear it."

A tear slipped down her cheek, and he caught it with his thumb. "You can't promise that."

His lips brushed over hers, the kiss slow, reverent. "I can. And I will."

She curled into him, listening to the sound of his breathing, feeling the warmth of his skin, willing time to slow—to stretch this moment into eternity.

But dawn would come.

And fate would not wait for them.

The stillness of the night had become deceptive, a fragile peace that shattered with the sound of hurried footsteps echoing down the corridor. The flickering candlelight cast long shadows along the stone walls, stretching into darkness, making the approaching figure seem even more ghostly.

A sharp knock came at the door.

Nathaniel stirred first, his body tense, muscles coiling beneath the sheets. Evangeline was slower, still lost in the warmth of his skin against hers, the hazy remnants of their last night together lingering like a dream. But reality crashed in quickly. The urgency in the knock sent a prickle of unease through her spine.

Nathaniel sat up, already reaching for his trousers, his instincts sharpened by years of battle. "Who is it?"

The door flung open before an answer could be given.

Vivianne stood in the doorway, breathless, her hair loose from its usual bindings. The sheen of sweat on her forehead glistened under the dim light, and for the first time, Evangeline noticed real fear in her eyes.

"The assassin is already moving," she gasped, chest heaving. "They could strike at any moment."

Nathaniel didn't hesitate. In one fluid motion, he was on his feet, reaching for the sword resting against the chair near the fireplace. The steel glinted as he fastened the belt around his waist, his movements swift, precise.

Evangeline threw off the sheets, scrambling after him. "I'm coming with you."

"No." His response was immediate, his voice sharp. "You stay here."

She gritted her teeth. "You don't get to decide that."

Nathaniel turned to face her, his expression dark with worry. "This isn't a debate, Evangeline. If something happens—"

"If something happens, I'd rather be with you than waiting in the dark, wondering if you're still alive!" she snapped, stepping forward until she was right in front of him, eyes blazing. "You can tell me to stay behind all you want, but it won't stop me from following."

Nathaniel exhaled heavily, jaw tightening. He glanced at Vivianne, who watched them with wary impatience before dragging a hand through his hair. "Damn it, Evangeline," he muttered, then let out a breath. "Fine. Stay close."

Vivianne nodded toward the hall, urgency returning to her voice. "We need to move now. If we wait any longer, it'll be too late."

Nathaniel took Evangeline's hand, squeezing it just once before letting go. His fingers still felt warm against her skin, but his eyes were cold, sharp—full of the unspoken promise that he would kill anyone who dared to take her from him.

With that, they stepped into the corridor, the night stretching before them, uncertain and treacherous.

Chapter Eighteen

The estate was too quiet. Unnaturally so.

Nathaniel's grip tightened around the hilt of his sword as he and his men moved through the dimly lit corridors. Shadows danced along the walls, flickering with each pass of their lanterns. The air was thick with tension, each footstep too loud, too sharp against the silence.

"Something's not right," one of his men murmured, scanning the empty hall. "It's like the place is holding its breath."

Nathaniel nodded, his instincts screaming the same warning. He turned to another guard. "Search the servant's quarters. Look for anything that seems out of place."

The men moved with trained efficiency, sweeping through the rooms, checking doors, windows, and corners where danger might lurk. But the stillness remained unbroken, the night pressing in around them with an unnatural weight.

Then—

"Sir! Over here!"

Nathaniel spun toward the voice, already moving. One of his men stood in the doorway of a servant's chamber, holding something small and metallic between his fingers. A dagger.

"It was hidden beneath the floorboards," the guard said

grimly, turning the blade over. The steel gleamed in the low light, wicked and sharp. "Someone planted it here."

Nathaniel's stomach twisted. His eyes swept the room, taking in the undisturbed bedding, the neat stack of folded linens by the hearth. "Then someone inside let them in."

A crash echoed from further down the hall.

Nathaniel's blood turned ice-cold. He bolted toward the sound, his men right behind him, weapons drawn.

A broken window.

Cold night air rushed in, sending the curtains billowing like spectres in the dark. Glass shards glittered on the wooden floor, moonlight catching the jagged edges.

And footprints—muddy, damp, leading inside.

Nathaniel's pulse thundered. The realization hit like a blow to the chest.

He wasn't hunting the assassin.

The assassin was already inside.

And he was hunting *them*.

The air in Evangeline's chambers was unnervingly still. The only sound was the faint rustle of the curtains shifting with the breeze from the open window. The cold air sent a shiver down her spine, but it wasn't the night chill that unsettled her—it was the silence.

She stood near the bed, gripping a dagger so tightly her knuckles ached. Her breaths were slow, controlled, her ears straining for any sound beyond the quiet crackle of the dying fire.

She wasn't alone.

A creak.

Her grip tightened. The sound came from the far side of the room, near the wardrobe.

Another creak—closer this time.

Then, a shadow moved.

She spun just as a figure lunged from the darkness. The

assassin was fast—faster than she expected—but she had been ready.

She ducked beneath his reach and drove the dagger forward, catching his arm as he swung toward her. The blade bit deep, a sharp hiss of pain escaping the intruder's lips as blood seeped through his sleeve.

But he didn't stop.

With brutal efficiency, he wrenched the weapon from her grasp and twisted her arm behind her back, forcing her against the edge of the bed. Pain lanced through her shoulder, but she refused to cry out.

"Feisty," the man murmured, his breath hot against her ear. "I'll give you that."

Evangeline struggled, but his grip was unyielding.

"You should be grateful," he continued, voice low and smooth, almost amused. "I could make this painless. But Ashford... well. He wanted you to suffer first."

A sharp chill ran through her veins. Ashford.

The assassin shifted, adjusting his grip as he reached for something—a blade, a garrote, she didn't know. But the moment his hold loosened, she reacted.

She threw her head back, the sharp crack of her skull colliding with his nose sending a shock through both of them. He cursed, his grip faltering for the barest second, and she wrenched herself free, stumbling toward the fireplace.

Before she could reach for the poker, a shadow moved in the doorway.

Nathaniel.

But he was unarmed.

Nathaniel didn't think. He acted.

He launched himself at the assassin, knocking him away from Evangeline with sheer force. They hit the ground hard, rolling into the hallway, limbs tangling, bodies colliding with brutal impact.

The assassin was trained—his movements calculated,

precise. He twisted, landing a blow to Nathaniel's ribs before rolling to his feet in one smooth motion.

Nathaniel barely had time to brace before the next strike came. The assassin was fast—too fast. A dagger flashed in his hand, the steel glinting under the dim candlelight.

Nathaniel dodged, barely. The blade sliced through his shirt, grazing his side, but he didn't stop. He swung, catching the assassin's jaw with a brutal punch that sent him staggering.

Blood dripped from the assassin's mouth, but he only smiled. "You're predictable, Sinclair. That'll get you killed."

Nathaniel wiped the sweat from his brow, his breath ragged. "And you talk too much."

The assassin lunged.

Nathaniel ducked the first strike, but the second caught him—dagger sinking deep into his side. White-hot pain exploded through his ribs.

He gritted his teeth, refusing to go down. Instead, he used the momentum, grabbing the assassin by the wrist and wrenching the blade free, twisting the man's arm so hard he heard the crack of bone. The assassin let out a strangled sound of pain, but it wasn't enough.

Nathaniel stumbled back, pressing a hand to his bleeding side. He was losing too much blood.

The assassin smirked, despite his broken arm. "Looks like you won't make it to your duel after all."

A gunshot shattered the air.

The assassin's body jerked. His eyes went wide in shock before he crumpled to the ground, blood pooling beneath him.

Nathaniel turned, chest heaving.

Vivianne stood at the end of the hall, a smoking pistol in her shaking hands.

Her breath was ragged, her face pale. "I— I didn't—" She swallowed hard, lowering the gun. "I had to."

Evangeline rushed to Nathaniel's side, pressing her hands to his wound. "You're bleeding too much. We need to—"

Nathaniel caught her wrist, his grip weak but firm. "It's over."

But in his gut, he knew the truth.

This wasn't over at all.

This was only the beginning.

Blood pooled on the floor, glistening darkly in the dim candlelight. The scent of iron filled the hallway, thick and suffocating. Nathaniel staggered, bracing himself against the wall, his breaths ragged, each inhale a sharp lance of pain through his wounded side.

Evangeline was on him in an instant. "You're hurt. Nathaniel, sit down before—"

"I'm fine." His voice was hoarse, but his grip on her wrist was firm. He wasn't fine. He could barely stand. But right now, pain didn't matter.

The body of the assassin lay crumpled on the floor, lifeless. The smoke from Vivianne's pistol still curled in the air, the silence stretching unbearably thick around them.

Vivianne swallowed hard, lowering the gun. Her hands were trembling. "I... I didn't mean to kill him," she whispered. "I just—he would've—"

Nathaniel looked at her, his expression unreadable. "You saved my life."

She let out a shaky breath, nodding. "That doesn't make it easier."

Evangeline turned back to Nathaniel, pressing her hands to his wound, trying to stem the bleeding. "We need to get you to a physician. Now."

Nathaniel ignored her, his gaze fixed on Vivianne. "Tell me the truth. How did he get in?"

Vivianne hesitated before shaking her head. "I don't know. But I do know who sent him."

Evangeline froze. "Ashford."

Vivianne nodded grimly. "It was him. No more guessing, no more doubt. He wants you dead, Nathaniel. He wants *both* of you dead."

Nathaniel clenched his jaw, his body taut with barely restrained fury. His hand curled into a fist, bloodied fingers trembling with rage. "Then this isn't a duel anymore."

Evangeline looked up at him, her stomach twisting at the coldness in his eyes. "Nathaniel—"

"This is war."

The finality of his words settled over them, heavy as the night itself.

And for the first time, Evangeline feared what that meant.

The study was dimly lit, the faint glow of dawn still far from breaking over the horizon. The fire in the hearth had long since burned to embers, leaving the room cloaked in a heavy, brooding silence.

Nathaniel sat in the chair by the desk, a strip of linen clenched between his teeth as he tightened the bandage around his side. His fingers trembled, but whether from pain or something deeper, Evangeline couldn't tell.

She stood a few feet away, watching him. He was different now. Something in his eyes, in his posture, had changed.

He wasn't just angry.

He was dangerous.

Nathaniel exhaled sharply, adjusting the bandage with a hiss. "Ashford thinks he's already won."

Evangeline swallowed, voice barely above a whisper. "Nathaniel..."

He didn't look at her. Instead, he reached for the bottle of brandy on the desk and took a slow, measured sip. "This duel was never about honor. Not for him. It was always about control. About making sure I never had a chance to take you from him."

Evangeline stepped closer. "You don't have to do this."

He let out a hollow laugh, finally lifting his gaze to meet

hers. "Don't I? You heard Vivianne. This wasn't a warning. This wasn't a threat. This was an execution order. He sent that man to gut you like an animal. He was never going to let you go."

She had no response to that. Because he was right.

Nathaniel leaned back in his chair, his expression unreadable, but the weight of his fury coiled tight in his frame. "He doesn't deserve a fair fight. He doesn't deserve an easy death."

Evangeline's stomach twisted. "Nathaniel, listen to yourself—"

"No," he cut her off sharply, his voice like steel. "Listen to *me*. I was willing to fight him with rules. With honor. But now? He's made this a war. And I intend to win it."

Evangeline felt the room shrink around her. She had never feared Nathaniel before—not truly—but this wasn't the man she had fallen in love with. This was something else. This was a man willing to do whatever it took, no matter the cost.

"What happens after, then?" she asked, her voice barely steady. "If you kill him—what happens to you?"

Nathaniel didn't answer. He only looked at her, the firelight catching the cold glint in his eyes.

And for the first time, Evangeline wasn't sure she wanted to know the answer.

Chapter Nineteen

The morning was heavy with mist, the sun struggling to break through the veil of fog that clung to the earth. Each footstep against the dampened ground echoed in the hush of dawn, a steady march toward fate.

Nathaniel walked ahead, his shoulders squared, his expression unreadable. Despite the wound in his side, his stride was even, his resolve untouched. He was a man walking toward his destiny, unshaken, unyielding.

Behind him, Evangeline and Vivianne followed in silence. There was nothing to say. The weight of what was coming hung over them like a storm waiting to break.

Evangeline's hands curled into fists at her sides. She couldn't bear it. The quiet, the acceptance, the way Nathaniel moved as if he'd already resigned himself to the outcome of this duel. She sped up, falling into step beside him.

"Please," she murmured, her voice just above a whisper. "If you kill him, this will never end. More men will come for you. More challenges. More blood."

Nathaniel kept his gaze forward, his jaw tightening.

"Listen to me." She reached for his arm, forcing him to

stop. "Killing him won't bring peace. It will only drag you into something darker. You know that."

Finally, he looked at her. The cold determination in his eyes sent a shiver down her spine.

"Evangeline," he said quietly, "this isn't about peace. It's about making sure he never lays another hand on you again."

She sucked in a sharp breath. "Then make sure of it without becoming like him. I know you, Nathaniel. You fight with honor. You don't need to kill him."

A muscle twitched in his jaw, but he didn't answer.

Vivianne, who had kept her silence thus far, finally spoke. "He won't stop, Evangeline. You know that. He'll always find a way to come back."

Evangeline turned to her, frustration and fear warring inside her. "Then we ruin him another way. Publicly. Socially. But not like this."

Nathaniel exhaled slowly. "I won't make you any promises."

Her fingers curled tighter around his sleeve. "Then promise me this."

His gaze flickered, waiting.

"Promise me that after today, it ends. That whatever happens on that field, you walk away with me."

His features softened, just barely. He reached for her hand, squeezing it briefly before letting go.

"After today," he murmured, "I'm yours."

She wished she could believe that meant he would spare Ashford. But the darkness in his eyes told her he had already decided.

They walked on, the mist swallowing them whole.

The duelling grounds stretched vast and empty, a field once meant for noble sport now tainted by the weight of vengeance. The morning mist had barely lifted, and the air was thick with the hush of an expectant crowd—gentlemen, lords, and those who thrived on bloodshed masked as honor.

Nathaniel stood still, his hand resting lightly on the hilt of his sword. The ache in his side burned with every breath, but he pushed it aside, his focus locked entirely on the man standing across from him.

Ashford.

The duke smirked, exuding an air of false confidence, though his fingers twitched at his side. He had expected to hear of Nathaniel's death days ago. The fact that he had survived rattled him.

A steward stepped forward, his voice echoing across the field. "State your cause before the duel commences."

Nathaniel's voice rang out first, steady as steel. "For honor."

Ashford gave a mocking laugh before lifting his chin. "For justice. And for putting a traitorous whore in her place."

A sharp gasp rippled through the gathered onlookers. Evangeline's hands clenched at her sides, but Nathaniel reacted first.

His sword was drawn in a heartbeat, the tip glinting in the weak sunlight. "Draw your weapon, Ashford. I'll not waste another breath listening to filth."

Ashford grinned, drawing his own blade with slow, deliberate ease. "Touched a nerve, did I? Good."

The steward signalled, and the duel began.

Ashford moved first, striking with surprising speed, forcing Nathaniel to parry immediately. The sound of steel meeting steel echoed across the field, sharp and ringing. The first exchange was clean, each man testing the other's reflexes, their footwork careful, precise.

Then Ashford played his first dirty trick.

As they circled each other, Ashford abruptly kicked up a spray of dirt and dust directly at Nathaniel's face.

Nathaniel flinched, barely dodging the follow-up thrust aimed at his exposed shoulder. He recovered swiftly, but a smirk pulled at Ashford's lips. "Oh dear. Did the honourable Lord Sinclair not see that coming?"

Nathaniel answered with a brutal lunge, forcing Ashford back.

But Ashford wasn't done. He pivoted sharply, his blade slicing low—too low—directly at Nathaniel's wounded side.

Pain lanced through Nathaniel as the gash reopened. Blood darkened his shirt. He staggered a step, his grip tightening around his sword.

"Predictable," Ashford taunted, eyes gleaming with amusement. "You shouldn't have come here wounded. It's hardly a fair fight."

"You wouldn't know a fair fight if it bled out at your feet," Nathaniel spat, his voice laced with fury.

Before he could retaliate, a sudden movement caught his eye. Ashford's second—his assistant—was moving toward him, stepping forward subtly as if adjusting position.

Nathaniel saw it too late.

The man kicked at Nathaniel's sword, knocking it from his grip.

The crowd gasped as Nathaniel was left unarmed, Ashford's blade gleaming, poised to strike.

The air around the duelling grounds crackled with tension. Nathaniel was outnumbered, unarmed, and bleeding, yet the judges stood motionless. The crowd whispered in hushed murmurs, but no one dared step forward.

Evangeline couldn't take it.

She stepped past the barrier of spectators, her voice slicing through the heavy silence. "He's cheating! You all see it!"

A ripple of murmurs ran through the gathered nobles. Some nodded in agreement, others shook their heads, muttering about how "a lady should not interfere."

One of the stewards turned sharply toward her. "Lady Evangeline, this is highly improper—"

"Improper?" she hissed, her hands trembling at her sides. "What is improper is allowing a man to fight with honor while his opponent stoops to cowardice and trickery! Are you all so blind that you would call this a duel?"

Ashford, blade still poised at Nathaniel's chest, smirked. "How adorable," he mocked, tilting his head. "Your little whore is speaking for you now, Sinclair? How much more shame will you suffer before you—"

The sharp click of a pistol hammer cut through the air.

Vivianne stepped forward, drawing all eyes as she raised her pistol and levelled it at Ashford's second.

"Intervene again," she said, her voice deadly calm, "and you die where you stand."

Gasps erupted from the crowd. A noblewoman shrieked, and several men stepped back in alarm. The second, caught mid-motion to assist Ashford once more, froze, his eyes darting between Vivianne and Ashford.

Ashford's expression darkened, a flicker of uncertainty flashing across his face.

Nathaniel, breathing hard, locked eyes with Evangeline. He saw the fire in her gaze, the sheer force of her will, and something inside him surged with renewed strength.

Ashford might have stacked the game in his favour, but he had underestimated them.

And now, for the first time, he was no longer in control.

The crowd held its breath, the weight of the moment pressing down like a vice. The duel had been brutal, and yet, against all odds, Nathaniel was still standing.

Fuelled by raw fury and sheer determination, he side-stepped Ashford's next reckless lunge, twisting his body just enough to send the duke stumbling forward. Ashford's blade slashed through empty air. The momentum carried him off balance, his boots slipping against the damp earth. He barely managed to catch himself before Nathaniel advanced again, pressing forward with ruthless precision.

Nathaniel's movements were slower now, pained but deliberate. Blood seeped through the fabric of his shirt, but he refused to falter. The fire in his gaze burned hotter than the pain lancing through his side.

Ashford snarled, his face contorted with rage. "You should be dead."

Nathaniel didn't respond. He struck again, their blades clashing with a screech of steel, the force of it sending Ashford reeling. The duke gritted his teeth, regaining his footing, but the shift in the battle was undeniable.

Nathaniel was winning.

The crowd murmured, nobles shifting uncomfortably as they watched Ashford falter. The fear in his eyes betrayed him—this wasn't how it was supposed to go.

Desperation bled into Ashford's next attack, his blade swinging wildly, but Nathaniel was waiting. He dodged, turning his body just enough to catch Ashford off guard before delivering a brutal strike to the duke's wrist.

Ashford cried out as his sword was sent flying. The blade hit the dirt with a hollow thud.

He fell to the ground, scrambling backward, his breathing ragged. He was defenceless.

Nathaniel stood over him, his own sword raised, the tip hovering just over Ashford's throat.

The entire world seemed to pause.

Evangeline could hear her own heartbeat pounding in her ears, her breath trapped in her chest as she watched Nathaniel—watched him teeter on the precipice of vengeance.

Ashford's chest heaved, his eyes wide, but even now, even on his knees, he refused to beg. Instead, he sneered. "Do it, then. Kill me, just like the brute everyone believes you to be."

Nathaniel didn't move. His grip on the hilt tightened.

"Nathaniel," Evangeline's voice was barely above a whisper. She took a step forward. "You don't have to do this."

His jaw clenched, but he said nothing.

"This isn't about him anymore," she continued, her voice thick with emotion. "It's about you. What kind of man do you want to be?"

Ashford's lips curled. "Listen to her, Sinclair. Let everyone see you hesitate. Let them see you weak."

Nathaniel exhaled slowly. The weight of every moment, every wound, every scar, bore down on him. The part of him that had sworn vengeance screamed for blood. The part of him that had spent his entire life chasing honor told him to stop.

He lowered his blade.

Ashford's breath hitched, his eyes narrowing in confusion. "What—"

Nathaniel turned to the gathered nobles, his voice steady and clear. "A man like this isn't worth dirtying my blade."

A ripple of gasps spread through the crowd. Whispers erupted, shock painting every face.

Ashford looked furious. "You—"

"You are ruined," Nathaniel cut him off coldly, his voice filled with finality. "You challenged me. You cheated. And you lost."

Ashford's face darkened, his humiliation sealing his fate before the entire ton.

Evangeline let out a breath she hadn't realised she was holding. Relief and admiration swelled within her as she looked at Nathaniel—her Nathaniel, the man who had fought for his honor and won, without losing himself in the process.

And Ashford, the man who had tormented them for so long, lay disgraced before the world.

Ashford remained where he had fallen, panting, dirt staining his once-pristine coat. Blood trickled from his split lip, his hand shaking as he pressed it against the grass for leverage. He was trying to rise, to salvage whatever dignity he could scrape together.

But the crowd had already turned against him.

A murmur spread among the gathered nobles, low at first but growing louder, swelling into an unmistakable sound of disapproval. Some averted their gazes in shame, while others—former allies, supposed friends—shook their heads, their expressions a mixture of disdain and disgust.

"A cheat," someone muttered.

"Coward," another voice scoffed.

Ashford's face burned with fury and humiliation, his breath coming fast and shallow as he tried to reclaim his composure.

Nathaniel stood above him, sword still in hand, but he did not strike. He did not have to.

"You are nothing," Nathaniel said at last, his voice carrying over the field. "You tried to take everything from me. You tried to destroy her. And now, look at you."

Ashford's hands curled into fists, his whole body trembling. "You think this is over?" His voice was raw, almost unhinged. "You think I will simply disappear?"

Nathaniel's gaze hardened. "You don't have a choice."

A ripple of laughter—harsh and unsympathetic—moved through the onlookers. The ton was not kind to losers, and even less so to those caught in disgrace. Whatever power Ashford had wielded over them, it was gone now.

Vivianne stepped forward, her movements slow and deliberate. The crowd hushed as she approached Ashford, her face unreadable. Then, in a single, calculated motion, she spat at the ground in front of him.

"You deserve worse," she said, her voice like ice. "But this will do."

Ashford flinched, his humiliation deepening.

A nobleman near the front turned away with a scoff. "Let's go. There's nothing more to see."

One by one, they began to leave. The lords and ladies of society—those who had once dined with Ashford, laughed at his jokes, sought his favour—walked away without another word. His downfall was complete.

Evangeline watched it all unfold, standing beside Nathaniel.

He had won.

And Ashford had lost everything.

Chapter Twenty

The carriage wheels rumbled softly against the dirt road, the silence inside suffocating. The duel was over. The war had ended. And yet, the weight of it all settled between them like an unspoken truth.

Evangeline sat beside Nathaniel, her hands folded in her lap, her fingers twisting together. She stole a glance at him—his face still taut with the remnants of battle, his hands stained with blood, his knuckles scraped raw. He stared out the window, the passing landscape a blur, his jaw set tight, his expression unreadable.

She had spent the last weeks fighting to keep him alive, to protect him from the forces conspiring against him. And now that the danger had passed, she found herself paralyzed, uncertain of what came next.

Tentatively, she reached for his hands.

Nathaniel didn't move at first. But after a moment, he turned to her, his gaze searching hers. She squeezed his hands lightly, silently thanking him—not for sparing Ashford, not for winning the duel, but simply for being here, still alive, still with her.

"It's done," she whispered, as if saying it aloud would make it feel real.

Nathaniel inhaled slowly, then exhaled just as deliberately. "It is."

But neither of them truly believed that was the end of it.

London pulsed with the aftermath of the duel. Gossip spread like wildfire through drawing rooms, gentlemen's clubs, and ballrooms alike. No one spoke of anything else. Some called Nathaniel a hero. Others whispered that he was a brute who should never have been allowed to return to society. The duel had not just settled a personal vendetta—it had fractured the very fabric of the ton.

Letters began arriving at Nathaniel's estate. Some were written in elegant script, offering praise and admiration.

You have done what many men would not have had the courage to do. Honor has been restored.

Others were less kind.

You have disgraced our world with your actions. Violence may have won you a duel, but it has lost you the respect of those who matter.

Nathaniel read each one without reaction before tossing them into the fire. He had expected nothing less.

Meanwhile, Vivianne was revelling in the downfall of the man who had once kept her in chains. Ashford's men had scattered, their loyalty dissolving the moment their master had fallen. The brothel—once a place of silent suffering—was finally hers, free of his grasp.

She lifted a glass of brandy in a quiet toast, her voice dry as she murmured, "A devil has fallen. But devils always have heirs."

The women around her murmured in agreement, a mixture of relief and wariness in their eyes. For now, they were safe.

But the shadows of men like Ashford never truly disappeared.

The estate was silent, wrapped in the deep hush of midnight. The world outside lay still, undisturbed. But inside Nathaniel's chambers, the darkness was anything but peaceful.

Nathaniel's breaths came in sharp, uneven gasps. His body was rigid, tangled in the sheets, his brow damp with sweat. Behind his closed eyelids, ghosts lurked—visions of Ashford's twisted smirk, the flash of a blade in the moonlight, the acrid scent of blood staining the duelling grounds.

He swung his sword, but no matter how many times he struck, Ashford did not fall. He laughed, his voice merging with the sneering faces of men long buried in Nathaniel's past. The duel blurred into every battle he had ever fought, every mistake he had ever made, every wound that had ever carved itself into his flesh.

Then Ashford lunged, his blade piercing Nathaniel's chest.

Nathaniel jolted awake with a strangled breath, his fingers clawing at the sheets as if to steady himself. His heart pounded against his ribs, his pulse wild. His hands, curled into fists, trembled violently in his lap.

He sat motionless, staring up at the ceiling, forcing himself to take in the stillness of the room—to remind himself that it was over. That Ashford was gone. That the war had been won.

But his body had not yet learned that truth.

Beside him, Evangeline stirred. She turned onto her side, blinking sleep from her eyes, her voice drowsy but laced with concern. "Nathaniel?"

He didn't respond immediately. He exhaled slowly, shaking his head, before he felt the warmth of her hand against his arm.

"Another nightmare?" she whispered.

He swallowed hard. "It was nothing. Go back to sleep."

She didn't. Instead, she sat up, her fingers sliding over his knuckles, still trembling from the lingering ghosts in his mind. "It's not nothing."

Nathaniel let out a bitter breath. "I should feel relieved. Victorious."

Evangeline squeezed his hand. "And do you?"

His silence was answer enough.

She shifted closer, resting her head against his shoulder, her warmth grounding him. "Even in victory, wounds don't heal overnight."

He gave a hollow chuckle, rubbing a hand over his face. "I don't know if they ever will."

Evangeline looked at him, her heart aching at the torment written in his expression. She had fought so hard to keep him alive, but she had not yet figured out how to bring him peace.

"Then we take it one night at a time," she whispered. "I'm here. Always."

Nathaniel exhaled, his body slowly relaxing, his fingers threading through hers.

For the first time since the duel, the weight on his chest lightened—just a little.

The morning after the duel was eerily quiet. The estate still stood, unchanged, as if the world hadn't just been reshaped by the clash of steel and blood. But inside Nathaniel's chambers, the air felt heavy with the ghosts of what had passed.

Evangeline sat by the window, staring out at the gray sky, the faintest drizzle misting over the grounds. The world moved on, uncaring of what they had endured. But she couldn't move on—not yet.

Nathaniel sat at the edge of the bed, rolling the bandages around his hand. His knuckles were raw, bruised from the fight. A wound on his side ached with every breath, but it wasn't the pain that troubled him. It was the silence.

Evangeline finally turned, watching him for a long moment before speaking. "Tell me, Nathaniel. What do we do now?"

Her voice was quiet, yet firm—demanding an answer he wasn't sure he had.

Nathaniel stopped, his hands resting in his lap. He exhaled slowly, as if weighing his words. And then, for the first time, he admitted the truth that had gnawed at him since the moment Ashford had fallen.

"I don't know."

The words landed between them, heavier than she had expected. Nathaniel Sinclair—the man who had always carried himself with confidence, who had fought tooth and nail to protect her—had no plan, no certainty of what came next.

Evangeline swallowed. "Neither do I."

He looked at her then, truly looked at her. The fire in her eyes, the strength that had carried them both through the darkest moments, was still there—but so was exhaustion, so was the weight of everything that had happened.

"This isn't a fairytale ending, is it?" she murmured.

Nathaniel huffed a breath of amusement, shaking his head. "No. It never was."

Silence stretched again, but this time it wasn't suffocating. It was understanding.

Evangeline crossed the room, standing before him. Slowly, carefully, she took his bruised hands in hers. "We're still here. That has to count for something."

Nathaniel studied her, something raw and unspoken in his gaze. "It does."

She nodded. "Then we take it one day at a time. Together."

His lips parted as if to speak, but instead, he pulled her into his arms. She melted into him, resting her cheek against his shoulder. And for the first time since the duel, since the fight for survival, they allowed themselves to simply exist in each other's presence.

The wounds would take time to heal. Some, perhaps, never fully would. But as long as they had each other, they had a future.

Whatever that might look like.

The gardens were still, touched by the first hints of dawn. Pale light filtered through the mist that clung to the hedges, turning the estate into something ethereal, something caught between night and morning. It was quiet, save for the distant rustle of the breeze through the branches.

Nathaniel and Evangeline sat side by side on a stone bench near the fountain, neither speaking, neither needing to. The silence between them wasn't tense, nor was it heavy with unsaid words. For the first time in what felt like years, it was simply peace.

Nathaniel's hand rested against his knee, fingers idly brushing over the fabric of his breeches. His body still bore the remnants of battle—bruises, stitches, healing wounds—but there was something different about him now. He wasn't just a man who had survived. He was a man searching for what came next.

Evangeline tilted her head, watching as he stared ahead, lost in thought. He looked different in this light, softer somehow. And yet, she could still see the weight of it all pressing on his shoulders.

Finally, he exhaled, glancing at her out of the corner of his eye. "Would you leave London with me?"

The question was quiet, but it cracked the morning stillness like a thunderclap.

Evangeline's breath caught in her throat. She turned to face him fully, searching his expression for meaning. "You want to leave?"

Nathaniel looked away, his jaw tightening. "I don't know if there's anything left for me here. The life I fought for... I don't know if it's what I want anymore."

Evangeline swallowed, her heart pounding. The weight of his words settled over her, warm and terrifying. Leaving London meant abandoning the world they knew. It meant forging something new, something entirely theirs.

Her fingers curled around the fabric of her dress, her mind racing.

Nathaniel turned back to her, his gaze steady but unreadable. "You don't have to answer now."

Evangeline opened her mouth, but no words came.

She simply looked at him, at the man she had fought for, the man who had fought for her in return.

The morning light stretched between them, waiting.

Chapter Twenty-One

The duelling grounds were hushed, the air thick with lingering tension. A moment ago, blades had clashed, a battle fought not just for honor but for something far more personal. Now, only the whispers of the crowd remained.

Ashford lay on the ground, his fine clothes stained with dirt and blood. The once-proud duke—now nothing more than a man broken in every way that mattered—struggled to rise. His chest heaved, but the weight of his defeat seemed too much to bear.

A pair of his men stepped forward, hesitant, unsure whether they should help him. No one else moved. No one cared to.

A nobleman standing near the front folded his arms and muttered, "He will never recover from this."

And that was the truth. Ashford was ruined.

Nathaniel stood above him, his sword still in his grasp, his breathing uneven. He had won. But as he stared down at the man who had nearly destroyed everything he loved, there was no satisfaction in his expression. No triumph. Just exhaustion.

Evangeline moved before she could stop herself.

She pushed past the onlookers, her feet barely touching the ground as she ran to Nathaniel. He barely turned before she reached him, her hands cupping his face, fingers trembling as they traced the bruises and cuts lining his skin.

"It's over," she breathed.

But even as she said it, she knew she was trying to convince herself as much as him.

Nathaniel exhaled, his forehead pressing against hers for the briefest moment. "Yes."

Behind them, the murmurs of the crowd grew. Lords and ladies exchanged glances, whispering about what this meant, how the balance of power had shifted. Some watched Ashford with pity, others with barely concealed delight.

But Evangeline paid them no mind.

Nathaniel had survived.

And for now, that was the only thing that mattered.

The carriage wheels rolled steadily against the dirt road, each turn bringing them closer to Nathaniel's estate. Yet inside, silence loomed heavier than the storm that had yet to break over London's skyline.

Evangeline sat rigidly, her hands folded in her lap, her fingers trembling against the fabric of her gown. She stared at them, unmoving, as if they weren't her own—as if she could still feel the ghost of the duel's aftermath upon them.

Nathaniel watched her carefully. He had seen her fight for her life, had seen her defy society's rules and stand against a man as dangerous as Ashford. Yet now, in the quiet of their carriage, she looked more shaken than she had on the duelling grounds.

Slowly, cautiously, he reached for her hand.

She flinched—barely—but enough that his fingers hesitated midair. Her breath hitched, and for a moment, she did not move. Then, just as carefully, she let her hand slip into his.

It was cold. Too cold.

Nathaniel squeezed gently, grounding her. "It's over," he murmured.

Evangeline finally looked at him, her throat tightening. "Is it?"

He had no answer to that. Not yet.

Meanwhile, in a separate carriage, Vivianne sat in silence, her fingers idly tracing the rim of her empty wine glass. The weight of the night pressed heavily upon her, but unlike Nathaniel and Evangeline, it was not fear or sorrow that clouded her mind.

It was realization.

She was free.

For the first time in years, she was free from Ashford's grasp. His men had scattered, his power crumbling like sand slipping through desperate fingers. She had spent so long surviving, manoeuvring around his control, that she had never dared to dream of a life beyond it.

Now, that life was hers to claim.

Vivianne smirked to herself, turning her gaze to the distant horizon.

Perhaps, at last, her story could begin anew.

By dawn, London was in uproar.

The duel between Nathaniel Sinclair and Duke Ashford was all anyone spoke of—whispers trailed through the corridors of power, rippling from lavish breakfast tables to the shadowed corners of gentlemen's clubs. The city buzzed with speculation, scandal, and, most of all, the question of what would happen next.

Had Nathaniel Sinclair truly slain a duke? Or worse—had he left him ruined, stripped of his dignity, yet still alive to plot revenge?

Letters flooded into Nathaniel's estate before he had even finished dressing for the day. Some were perfumed, written in elegant, sloping script, offering admiration:

You have done what needed to be done. Honor has been restored.

Others carried a more venomous bite:

Violence begets violence, my lord. A man who slays a duke today may find himself in the grave tomorrow.

Nathaniel barely spared them a glance before tossing them into the fire.

Evangeline, seated across from him in the drawing room, watched the flames curl around the letters, consuming them one by one. "Do they anger you?" she asked, her voice quieter than usual.

Nathaniel exhaled through his nose. "No. They bore me."

She studied him, noting the tension still wound tight in his jaw, the way his hands curled slightly even when relaxed. His duel may have been won, but the battle inside him had yet to settle.

A sharp knock at the door drew their attention. The butler entered, his expression carefully neutral, but the way he held the envelope suggested something more weighty than mere gossip.

"A decree, my lord. From the King."

Evangeline's breath caught.

Nathaniel took the envelope, breaking the wax seal with a flick of his thumb. His eyes scanned the words before he passed the letter to her. "It seems His Majesty has made a decision."

Evangeline's gaze darted over the parchment, her heart hammering. If Ashford had been spared, then...

By decree of His Majesty, Duke Ashford is hereby stripped of his title, his holdings forfeit to the Crown.

A shuddering breath escaped her lips. "It's done."

Nathaniel tilted his head slightly. "Is it?"

London would not forget the duel so easily. The scandal would linger. But at least one thing was certain—Ashford, whether dead or disgraced, would never again have the power to hurt them.

The sun had begun to set over Nathaniel's estate, casting long golden streaks through the grand windows. The warmth of the light did little to soften the chill in the air as Vivianne stood by the entrance hall, a small satchel in hand, her traveling cloak fastened tightly at her throat.

Evangeline lingered at the base of the staircase, her fingers twisting idly in the fabric of her gown. A part of her had expected Vivianne to stay—to weave herself into the life they had fought so hard to reclaim. But she should have known better. Vivianne had never been the kind to linger where she no longer belonged.

"You're truly leaving?" Evangeline asked, her voice softer than she had intended.

Vivianne smirked, tilting her head. "You sound surprised. I was never meant for a quiet life in the countryside. And London?" She exhaled sharply. "London will always reek of Ashford to me."

Evangeline lowered her gaze. She understood that more than she cared to admit.

Vivianne stepped forward and, to Evangeline's surprise, pressed something cold and smooth into her palm. Evangeline looked down, her breath catching—a dagger, small but expertly crafted, gleamed in the dim light. Its hilt was adorned with intricate silver etching, a weapon as beautiful as it was deadly.

"Vivianne—"

"No," Vivianne interrupted, her expression unreadable. "You don't need to be rescued anymore. You never did, not really. But now, no one will ever doubt it. Not even you."

Evangeline swallowed hard, her fingers tightening around the hilt. The gesture meant more than words ever could.

Then, before she could second-guess herself, she did something that startled them both—she stepped forward and embraced Vivianne.

For a moment, Vivianne stiffened. Then, with a small exhale, she returned the hug, her arms strong but careful.

"Take care of yourself," Evangeline whispered.

Vivianne pulled back first, her smirk returning, but there was something gentler in her gaze. "Always."

Nathaniel, who had watched the exchange silently, finally stepped forward. His expression was unreadable, his usual guarded nature firmly in place. But when he spoke, his voice carried a rare sincerity. "Thank you."

Vivianne arched a brow. "For what?"

His gaze flickered to Evangeline before returning to Vivianne. "For saving her life."

Vivianne shrugged, but her smirk softened. "What can I say? I have a habit of ruining men's plans. Ashford's, yours... it's a talent."

Nathaniel exhaled a quiet laugh, shaking his head.

She turned, pulling the hood of her cloak over her head. "Try not to get yourselves killed. I'd hate to return to London just to clean up your mess."

And with that, Vivianne stepped out into the cool evening, disappearing into the fading light.

Evangeline let out a slow breath, clutching the dagger to her chest.

"She's truly gone," she murmured.

Nathaniel watched the doorway for a long moment before responding. "She was never meant to stay."

And somehow, Evangeline knew he was right.

The sky was streaked with the dying light of the sun, bleeding hues of amber and rose into the horizon. The gardens, once the backdrop of so many whispered arguments and stolen moments, now held a quiet serenity. Evangeline sat on the stone bench, hands clasped in her lap, staring ahead but seeing nothing.

For the first time in what felt like forever, the future stretched before her, uncertain and unclaimed.

The soft crunch of boots against gravel pulled her from her thoughts. She didn't need to turn to know it was Nathaniel. He hesitated just before reaching her, as if debating whether or not to intrude.

"You can sit," she murmured.

Nathaniel took the invitation, lowering himself onto the bench beside her. They sat in silence, the cool evening air settling around them like a second skin.

"It feels different," Evangeline finally said. "Not having to fight. Not having to run."

Nathaniel nodded, though he seemed equally adrift. "It does."

Another stretch of quiet. Then, he exhaled, turning slightly to face her. "Evangeline... I don't want to assume anything. Not about us. Not about what comes next."

She looked at him then, her heart tightening at the uncertainty in his expression. This was the same man who had fought for her, who had killed and bled and sacrificed. And yet, now, in this moment, he was offering her something she had never been given before.

A choice.

Nathaniel reached for her hand, brushing his fingers over hers. "I will love you no matter what comes next. But tell me—where do you want our story to go?"

Evangeline parted her lips, but no words came. For so long, her life had been dictated by others—by duty, by scandal, by survival. But now, she stood at the threshold of something entirely new, something terrifying in its openness.

She turned her gaze back to the horizon, watching as the last light of day faded into dusk.

For the first time in her life, the choice was hers alone.

Chapter Twenty-Two

The morning light filtered through the grand windows of Nathaniel's estate, casting long golden beams across the polished wooden floors. The world outside was still, untouched by the chaos that had defined their lives for so long.

Evangeline woke to the softness of silk sheets against her skin, but the space beside her was empty.

Nathaniel was gone.

For a fleeting moment, panic stirred in her chest, but then she saw it—the slight indentation in the mattress where he had been. He had left quietly, without waking her. Giving her space. Letting her think.

She exhaled and stretched, pressing her palms against her face.

What now?

The question had followed her all night, turning over in her mind until exhaustion finally claimed her. She had spent so much of her life fighting, running, surviving. Now, with the battle won and the past buried, she found herself unmoored. She had always known what she was running from—but had never stopped to ask herself what she was running toward.

She slid out of bed, wrapping herself in the dressing robe that had been laid neatly across the chair. The estate was unusually quiet, a rare peace settling over it like a soft blanket. As she wandered through the halls, she let her fingers trail along the familiar walls, each step feeling heavier than the last.

When she reached her vanity, she stopped. Something was waiting for her.

A sealed letter.

She hesitated before picking it up, recognising the elegant, sharp handwriting before she had even broken the seal.

Vivianne.

Her pulse quickened. She had said her goodbyes—what more was there to say? But as she unfolded the letter, she found herself holding her breath.

Evangeline,

Freedom is a strange thing. It is both a gift and a burden, and it is never given—it must always be taken. You have the power now. Don't waste it.

For years, I convinced myself that I had no choices. That I was merely surviving, doing what I had to do. But survival is not the same as living, and I suspect you know that better than most.

There was a time when I might have envied you. Now, I only hope you make the choice I never could. Do not let fear tether you to the past. Do not let guilt make you stay where you do not belong. Choose what you want, Evangeline. Not what is expected of you. Not what is safe.

And if that choice is love, then take it fiercely and without regret.

If I have learned anything, it is this—hesitation is its own kind of cage.

Don't lock yourself inside it.

—Vivianne.

Evangeline's fingers tightened around the parchment, her

breath unsteady. The inked words blurred slightly, not from the light but from the emotions welling behind her eyes.

She had spent so long searching for escape, for control over her own fate. But Vivianne was right—what was the point of freedom if she didn't claim it?

Her heart knew the answer before her mind had fully caught up.

With newfound resolve, she stood, smoothing the creases from her gown. She folded the letter carefully and placed it inside the drawer of her vanity, as if tucking away a part of herself for safekeeping.

Then, without another second of doubt, she turned on her heel and left the room.

She was going to find Nathaniel.

The gardens were bathed in the soft glow of the afternoon sun, a golden hue painting the hedgerows and flowerbeds with a dreamlike serenity. A gentle breeze whispered through the leaves, stirring the air with the scent of late-blooming roses.

Evangeline's heart pounded as she stepped onto the stone pathway, her hands curling into fists at her sides. She had made her decision. Now, she had to see it through.

Nathaniel was there, standing near the fountain, his back to her. His posture was tense, hands clasped behind him as though bracing himself. As if he, too, was waiting for an answer he feared.

She took a breath, gathering the last of her resolve. "Nathaniel."

He turned, his gaze locking onto hers. In that instant, she saw it all—the uncertainty, the hope, the love he was barely holding back. And she knew she had made the right choice.

She didn't hesitate.

She walked straight toward him, stopping only when there was barely a breath of space between them.

Nathaniel swallowed hard, his throat bobbing. "Did you—"

"Yes," she interrupted, voice trembling but sure. "But on my terms."

Nathaniel stilled, his breath catching. Then, after a moment, he exhaled, the weight of his tension melting from his shoulders. He reached for her hands, taking them gently in his own.

"Evangeline," he said, voice low but steady, "marry me. Not because of Ashford. Not because of scandal. But because there is no future I want where you are not by my side."

Tears pricked at the corners of her eyes. She had been waiting for this—not an obligation, not a duty, but a choice. One she could make freely, without fear.

She squeezed his hands, her lips curling into a small, trembling smile. "Yes."

Nathaniel's relief was almost palpable. He let out a shaky laugh, pressing a lingering kiss to her knuckles before pulling her into his arms, holding her as though he never intended to let go.

And for the first time in her life, Evangeline truly believed she was free.

The terrace was bathed in the golden hues of twilight, the last remnants of the sun dipping below the horizon. A warm breeze stirred the leaves, carrying the faint scent of lavender and jasmine. Evangeline stood at the balustrade, gazing over the gardens, deep in thought.

Nathaniel stepped onto the terrace behind her, his footsteps quiet against the stone floor. He didn't speak immediately, simply observing her in the fading light. When she finally turned, her eyes met his with an intensity that sent a shiver down his spine.

"I won't have our marriage be like others," she said softly, but firmly. "I won't be a wife locked away in a grand house with nothing but gossip and embroidery to fill my days."

Nathaniel's lips quirked in amusement. "You never struck me as the idle sort."

She stepped toward him, voice unwavering. "I want purpose, Nathaniel. I want more than a title and a place on your arm. I've spent too much of my life being controlled by the will of others. If I marry you, it will be because I choose it —on my terms."

Nathaniel exhaled, a slow smile forming. "I never wanted to take away your freedom, Evangeline."

She searched his face for any sign of hesitation, but all she found was quiet conviction. "Then we must leave London," she continued. "At least for a while. Start somewhere new, somewhere away from the whispers of the ton and the ghosts of what we've endured."

Nathaniel took her hands in his, squeezing gently. "Wherever you wish to go, we will go. As long as I have you, nothing else matters."

Evangeline's heart clenched. For the first time, she felt the weight of possibility—not just survival, not just escape, but a life of her own making.

She smiled, feeling lighter than she had in years. "Then we leave."

Nathaniel leaned in, pressing his forehead against hers. "Together."

And just like that, their future belonged to them alone.

The night was quiet, save for the faint whisper of the wind against the windows. Inside the dimly lit study, the fire crackled softly, casting golden hues across the room. It was just the two of them now—no more expectations, no more prying eyes. Only them.

Evangeline turned the ring between her fingers, watching how the firelight caught the smooth metal, how it shimmered like something alive. She had worn a ring once before, but never like this. Never with this choice.

Nathaniel stood before her, watching her with quiet intensity. "Are you certain?" he asked, voice rough with emotion. "If we leave, there's no going back."

She lifted her eyes to his, steady, unyielding. "I was never meant to go back."

Nathaniel exhaled, reaching for her hand. His fingers trembled slightly as he slid the ring onto her finger—not as a claim, not as a demand, but as a vow. "This is my promise to you."

Evangeline, feeling the weight of the moment, turned her hand over and clasped his, drawing it toward her chest. "And this is mine to you," she whispered. "This is not just your promise, Nathaniel. It is mine, too."

He smiled then, something raw and breathtaking, and in that instant, she knew—this was not an ending.

It was a beginning.

She lifted onto her toes, pressing her lips to his, sealing the vow between them. When she pulled away, her eyes shone with something new, something fierce.

"For the first time," she whispered, "my fate is mine to write."

Nathaniel traced his thumb along her jaw, his own smile forming. "Then let's write it together."

She laced her fingers through his, holding tight. "We are free. Together."

The fire crackled, the world outside quieted, and for the first time in her life, Evangeline felt truly, utterly whole.

Chapter Twenty-Three

The morning light streamed through the curtains, golden and soft, wrapping the room in quiet warmth. For the first time in years, Evangeline woke with no weight pressing on her chest, no lingering dread waiting for her in the corners of the room. There was no urgency, no expectation—just the simple sensation of waking in a world where she had chosen her own fate.

She stretched slowly, relishing the feeling of the linen sheets against her skin, the stillness of a house that no longer felt like a prison. A faint sound drifted up from below—laughter. Low and rich, followed by the clinking of dishes. Nathaniel.

Evangeline smiled to herself as she sat up, running a hand through her hair. The house, which had once felt so cold, now hummed with something lighter. The weight of the past was gone—no longer lingering in the walls, no longer dictating their future.

She dressed without the aid of maids, without corsets cinched too tightly or gowns chosen for propriety's sake. She laced her own bodice, fastened her own skirts, and let her hair fall loosely over her shoulders. Today, she dressed for herself.

As she made her way downstairs, the scent of warm bread and fresh coffee filled the air. She reached the doorway to the dining room and paused, leaning against the frame.

Nathaniel stood at the table, speaking easily with one of the older servants, his shirt sleeves rolled up, his expression open and unguarded. He looked different in the daylight—lighter, freer. As if, for the first time, he was no longer carrying the world alone.

He caught sight of her and his lips curved into a slow, knowing smile. "Good morning, wife-to-be."

Evangeline crossed the room, unable to keep from smiling as she stood beside him. "Good morning, husband-to-be."

Nathaniel reached for her hand, pressing a kiss to her knuckles before turning back to the table. "I hope you're hungry. The cook insisted on celebrating our engagement."

She glanced at the spread—fresh fruit, eggs, warm scones, and sweet preserves. The simple luxury of a peaceful breakfast together was something she had never thought to have. Not like this.

Evangeline pulled out a chair, settling into the moment. "I could get used to this."

Nathaniel poured her a cup of coffee, watching her over the rim of his own. "That's the idea."

For a long time, they simply sat together, speaking in quiet tones, sharing small smiles, and letting the world settle into place around them. No grand declarations, no elaborate plans—just the certainty that they had survived, that they had won.

Evangeline set her cup down, reaching for Nathaniel's hand across the table. "We are free. Together."

Nathaniel gave her fingers a gentle squeeze. "Always."

And for the first time, there was no battle left to fight. No war left to win.

Only the life they had chosen.

Only the beginning of everything to come.

The late morning sun bathed the gardens in a warm,

golden glow as Evangeline stepped outside. The air was crisp, carrying the scent of roses and freshly turned earth. She let her fingers trail over the petals of a nearby flower as she walked, savoring the quietude.

Nathaniel was already there, leaning casually against a large oak tree, watching her approach with that ever-familiar smirk.

"You're staring," she teased, coming to a stop beside him.

"I like what I see," he countered, reaching out to tuck a loose strand of hair behind her ear. "You look... content."

She tilted her head, considering. "I think I am."

They stood in silence for a moment, watching as the breeze rustled the leaves, the world around them feeling lighter than it had in years.

"Are you ready for a life without war?" she finally asked, a playful challenge in her tone.

Nathaniel chuckled. "Only if it's with you."

She let out a breath, shaking her head at him. "You're impossible."

"I prefer relentless."

They walked together, side by side, the gravel crunching softly beneath their feet. There was no need to rush, no battle to prepare for—just this. A slow, steady rhythm that belonged to them alone.

Nathaniel glanced at her, eyes filled with something unspoken. "We don't have to decide everything right away, Evangeline. We can take our time."

She looked up at him, surprised. He had always been so decisive, so certain in everything. And yet, here he was—offering her space, freedom, choice.

She exhaled, a smile tugging at her lips. "Then let's take our time."

Nathaniel laced his fingers through hers, squeezing gently. "Together."

And for once, there was no rush. No looming fate. Just the promise of tomorrow, waiting for them to step into it.

The flickering candlelight cast a golden glow across the small room, the scent of roses and fresh parchment lingering in the air. There were no grand decorations, no audience of noblemen waiting with judgmental eyes. Just the quiet hum of a love that had endured every storm.

Evangeline stood before Nathaniel, her heart steady, her hands warm in his. There was no priest, no extravagant ceremony—only them, and the promises they chose to make.

Nathaniel's voice was low, filled with reverence as he spoke. "For every moment you have fought for yourself, for every choice that has been stolen from you—I vow that you will never have to fight alone again."

Evangeline swallowed past the lump in her throat, her fingers tightening around his. "I vow to love you—not because I must, not because I should, but because I choose to. Every day, for the rest of my life."

His lips parted slightly, as if caught off guard by the depth of her words, but he said nothing—just reached for the ring. The same one he had given her before, the one she had worn with hesitation, with fear.

This time, when he slid it onto her finger, she met his gaze without doubt, without hesitation.

Nathaniel let out a slow breath, brushing his thumb over her knuckles. "You are mine, and I am yours. In every way that matters."

Evangeline lifted her hand, pressed her palm against his heart. "This is not just your promise, Nathaniel. It is mine, too."

A long silence stretched between them, filled only with the steady rhythm of their breathing, of the moment settling in their bones.

Nathaniel exhaled, a rare, boyish grin breaking across his face. "Well then, Lady Sinclair, what shall we do with forever?"

She laughed, the sound bright and boundless. "Live it."

And with that, he kissed her—soft and slow, as if sealing every vow into her very soul.

They were no longer bound by duty, by scandal, by fear.

Only love.

And for the first time, their future was truly their own.

The fire crackled softly, casting warm golden light across the dimly lit room. Evangeline sat curled up on the plush settee, her fingers wrapped around a delicate glass of brandy. The weight of the day had finally settled, leaving behind an exhaustion that was not unwelcome—but a quiet kind, the kind that came after long battles had been fought and won.

Nathaniel sat across from her, his long legs stretched out before him, one arm draped lazily over the back of his chair. His eyes, softened by the flickering light, watched her with quiet contemplation.

"You're thinking about something," he murmured, swirling the amber liquid in his glass. "I can see it."

Evangeline exhaled, a small smile tugging at the corners of her lips. "You always see too much."

He tilted his head, waiting. Patient, as always.

She let the silence stretch between them for a moment before speaking, her voice softer than she had intended. "I still want to leave London for a while."

Nathaniel's gaze didn't waver, nor did he look surprised. Instead, he nodded, as if he had expected it. "Then we leave at first light."

Evangeline blinked, caught off guard by how quickly he agreed. "Just like that?"

Nathaniel leaned forward, resting his elbows on his knees. "Evangeline, I have never fought to keep you in a place where you did not wish to be." His voice was steady, certain. "London has never been kind to you. If you want to leave, then we leave."

She swallowed past the sudden tightness in her throat,

looking away. "And what about you? Your responsibilities, your estate—"

"My estate will still stand," he interrupted gently. "And whatever responsibilities I have, I will handle them in time." His lips curved into a slow smile. "It seems to me that, for once, we have the luxury of deciding our own fate."

Evangeline studied him, her heart tightening in a way that was both painful and beautiful. She had spent so long fighting —against the world, against expectations, against herself. And yet here he was, offering her the very thing she had never thought possible.

A choice.

A future of her own making.

She set her glass aside and crossed the room, standing before him. Nathaniel watched her carefully, his hand coming up to rest at her waist as she stepped between his knees.

"And where will we go?" she whispered, her fingers tracing the fine stitching of his waistcoat.

"Wherever you want," he murmured, his thumb brushing against her hip. "Somewhere warm. Somewhere far away. Or perhaps somewhere quiet, where no one knows our names."

She closed her eyes briefly, leaning into his touch. The fire crackled beside them, the scent of smoke and aged leather filling the air.

She had chosen her life. She had chosen her future.

And as Nathaniel pressed a kiss to her wrist, she knew, with absolute certainty, that she had chosen right.

The night stretched long and quiet, the weight of the world finally slipping away. A cool breeze drifted through the open balcony doors, the sheer curtains billowing like ghostly silk. The scent of rain lingered in the air, mixing with the warmth of candle wax and faint embers still glowing in the fireplace.

Evangeline lay against Nathaniel's chest, her fingers idly tracing the pendant that rested against his skin. A token of a past neither of them could erase, a reminder of a night filled with desperation, love, and fear. But it was also proof—proof that they had survived, that they had chosen each other again and again despite everything.

Nathaniel's hand smoothed slow circles against her back, his breathing steady. He had been quiet for some time, but not in the way that meant he was lost in thought. No, this was different. It was contentment.

"You're awake," he murmured, voice rough from sleep.

She hummed in response, still tracing the cool metal of the pendant. "I was thinking."

His chest vibrated with a low chuckle. "I can feel it."

Evangeline smiled against his skin. "Do you regret any of it?"

Nathaniel didn't answer right away, and for a moment, she feared his silence. But then he tightened his hold on her, pressing a lingering kiss to the crown of her head.

"Not a single moment," he said firmly. "Not even the worst of it. Because it brought me here."

She exhaled softly, closing her eyes. "We have spent so long fighting fate," she whispered. "Only to find that we had been meant for each other all along."

Nathaniel stilled beneath her words, and then slowly, carefully, he rolled onto his side, bringing them face to face. His hand slid along her jaw, his thumb brushing across her cheek as he searched her eyes.

"I would do it all again," he admitted, his voice lower now, reverent. "Every mistake, every hardship, every battle—if it meant finding my way back to you."

Evangeline swallowed hard, overwhelmed by the truth in his gaze. She had fought him, doubted him, doubted herself—but here they were. Alive. Together.

Finally free.

She reached up, pressing her palm over his heart, feeling

the steady beat beneath her fingers. "The war is over," she whispered, voice trembling. "And we have won."

Nathaniel exhaled, a slow, easy smile tugging at his lips. He leaned in, his forehead resting against hers, their breaths mingling. "Yes," he murmured, sealing the words between them with a kiss. "We have."

And for the first time, their story was no longer written by fate.

It was theirs to create.

About the Author

Kiana Aspen is a passionate storyteller who weaves romance, tension, and intrigue into every tale she writes. With a love for historical and darkly seductive narratives, she crafts stories that explore power, love, and the delicate line between ruin and redemption.

Her novel, *Masaki's Submission*, is an intense and emotionally charged romance that delves into themes of control, devotion, and the boundaries of desire. It's a story of power dynamics, unspoken longing, and the undeniable connection between two souls who find solace in surrender.

The Shadows of Desire is a tale of seduction, deception, and a love that thrives in the darkness. With an irresistible blend of passion and danger, this book explores the hidden desires that lurk beneath carefully crafted facades—and what happens when secrets become impossible to hide.

Kiana deeply values her readers and their feedback. If you enjoyed *The Duke's Ruin*, leaving a review would mean the world to her. Reviews not only help other readers discover her books but also allow her to grow as a writer and continue creating the stories you love.

Follow Kiana for updates and exclusive content:
TikTok: @kianaaspenauthor
Email: kianaaspenbooks@gmail.com

Printed in Great Britain
by Amazon